Shaman Wheel

Gene Smithson

803 Lambeth Lane

Austin Texas 78748

waldosmithson@yahoo.com

Cover and interior design by Amrit Khalsa and Gene Smithson

First Edition

ISBN: 9798514029921

Disclaimer

This is a work of **fiction**. Unless otherwise indicated, all the names, characters, businesses, places, events and incidents in this **book** are either the product of the author's imagination or used in a fictitious manner. Any resemblance to actual persons, living or dead, or actual events is purely coincidental.

The Shaman Wheel

Medicine Woman

by

Gene Smithson

PROLOGUE

Family

The early morning sun peeks over the mountain's ridge, bathing the valley below in a warm, golden light. Ponderosa pine, tall, rusty-red giants, litter the sides of the sloping, bending land and beneath them, pine needles drift like snow, only warm, dry and brown.

A young man slips silently down slope, carefully watched by the sentinel trees. The giant trees stand half in the here, half in the heavens, with so many years stored in their tribe's collective memory, that this moment blurs into many others, decades, even centuries past.

This ancient highland valley is beautiful, and powerful in a honey rich and thick way, but no one stays here for long. Pinecones, hanging restless in the trees, rustle and rub with every shift of the wind, crafting an eerie, jittery sort of song. Enormous white clouds chase across the vast blue sky like angels frightened into flight and fleeing. The swaying, rocking, up and down branches of the enormous old trees, and the golden-brown grasses whisper their own uncomfortable magic. It is always windy here.

Perched high above, giant raven critique and call, never pleased with what they see. Or so it seems to the young man.

The sun's warmth weighs heavy on his skin. His black hair shines. The young man treads soft and sure, moving down to the snow melt stream that is gurgling happily over rock. Straight reeds line the bank and sway and scuff, one against another, lending an accompaniment and substance to the lighter, happier, bubbling sounds of water. Away and overhead, the sky is blue enough to hurt his eyes. The faintest hint of smoke swirls and snakes all round, teasing his mind with promises of warmth and home, soft furs and play.

The young man suddenly stops and kneels. Reaching for the pouch hanging round his neck, he pulls a pinch of tobacco and flings it to the four directions, giving thanks for his safe return. The journey was far this time and long or so it seemed. The dirt of this world clings to his skin, a separation of sorts, that must be lost, left out here, before he is with her.

The young man will strip and wash and scrub with black sand scooped from the stream's dark glittery bottom; the frigid water will burn his skin and his sins will fall away and wash down stream like leaves large and small, detritus drifting to wherever it is that sins go.

Entering the clear icy water, the young man's nostrils flare and his spine goes straight, but the soft skin around his eyes never tightens. Easing farther down into the water, one small involuntary gasp escapes through his lips and Raven, with his shiny critical eye takes note. Expressions of surprise or discomfort are not allowed; Raven takes flight and squawks his shrill disapproval.

The young man, puny and grounded as he imagines himself to be, laughs aloud...the raven may fly but he knows not love. Surely if he did, he would not waste his time here critiquing the Young Man's bath.

Some moaning movement of air through the branches of the fallen silvery, white birch that straddles the creek is followed by shadow. Young Man feels it inside himself. It is a thin layer of dust settling over some shiny mirror and his joy is just dimmed, just intruded upon, just touched by some barely perceived intuition.

One more splash and up on the bank, he slaps droplets from his chilled skin with his icy, wrinkled hands and sends out something, some searching awareness, some intention directed. When his seeking searching sense lands on nothing, he whistles his mount over and leaps aboard. Scratching and rubbing and teasing his mount, Young Man sits tall and fiercely proud. Horse is his companion of many weeks, and they know one another as thoroughly as best friend brothers, comrades in all.

Young Man has only to look in the direction of home and Horse starts, and twitches his tail, and side hops with excitement. The horse knows where they go, and he feels the young man's excitement. He does not prance, he is far too practical for that, but he does dance and step light and high; and he does quiver and fill with such an urgent, happy energy that he can hardly be still. Young Man laughs and whoops and scrubs his friend's neck and they move up and along the soft, golden slope. There is the huffing bellows of the horse's breath and the up-down, in-out, forward-pause rocking, and the same rhythm finds the young man and they are as one creature, one purpose, one mind.

Young Man and Horse travel at an easy, rolling pace. The miles fall away like worries resolved. Riding just below the ridgeline, weaving through the trees their thoughts run ahead and Woman knows they come.

Home

For a long moment Young Man and Horse do not move. Horse stands knee deep in the cold creek water. Still as statues they both watch the woman.

Woman stands tall, watching back, her spine pointed up to sky, as straight as fire smoke on a windless day, as straight as a young tree or a well-made arrow's shaft. What thoughts pass between her, and Young Man cannot be known, but it is for some minutes that they stare without moving as the electric charge between them waves and pulses, builds and flows, like the great northern lights, clouds of magnetism and color.

As one, all break into violent motion, Young Man leaning into his mount's leap forward, Woman turning to run as hard as she can, towards the much too distant tree line. Fat droplets, white diamonds, froth round the painted pony's hooves and grasses fly from the woman's feet as she races fast as any prey ever. And the first *whoop!* erupts from the Young Man's throat as he and Horse clear the low bank in a running leap and close the gap. Woman glancing back with her laughing mouth and flashing eyes, runs harder, her soft brown skin rippling, her long slender legs pressing her forward like some wild animal cat, feline fast, ribs heaving, hair streaming.

Suddenly, Woman is lifted from the ground and carried. Her legs still churning the air, she is laughing aloud. The young man on the horse is growling as he lifts her with one arm, to seat her in front of him. His hands are tangled in mane, his arms around the woman. Horse is galloping for the sheer joy-freedom of it; he too is happy to be home.

Woman is leaning back, laying back, her arms flung wide, hands held open; she is trust and trusting. And she allows the young man warrior to hold her; keep her from falling. She is trusting, challenging and perhaps too, some sort of questioning surrender. Woman must ask, must know. Can the young man hold her wildness, whole and safe? And in this moment and for this moment, she allows and falls, into the space of completeness.

Horse skids to a huffing stop, bodies slide from his back and tumble, into the tall brown grasses that smell of sweet hay and lavender and smoke and earth and fertility and nurturing feminine-ness. The Great Mother is soft and as they land, Woman rolls and is on her back looking up. She is laughing with her mouth, but her eyes are hunting and hungry and her hands are moving, without guile, without hesitation, with the honest want of a wife for her man and he, Young Man, just as certain though not as deft, is reaching and pulling and forgetting and falling to press his thirsty lips against her neck and face and hair and wrist and everywhere he can find his woman's bare skin.

Two beings, both searching, seeking, wanting, finding, one plunge into familiar, the home, the oneness, and Woman gasps and now the young man is laughing, and, in this moment, there is a returning, a wholeness to them both. Young Man feels a warmth that has been gone for these long days and Woman feels a fear for loving so deep and full.

The two make sex as an exaltation, a profound affirmation, a YES, flung in the face of all uncertainty. In very short order, both Young Man and Woman cry out and fog into one, melt into One and melting into one, they sigh and whisper and question and laugh. Their eyes widen and soften and the two whole people gaze at each other in the sweetness of wonder.

Horse snorts his teasing approval, and the lovers laugh. Woman tousles her young warrior's hair, and he swells to tell of the success of the hunt and meat and supplies.

And too... there is some happy hidden story that Woman is not speaking, that the young man warrior cannot see, because Young Warrior, as are all men back, is too full of himself. Maybe tomorrow as they lay in blankets, entwined, and spun together, he will notice the softening of her belly and the secret she hides at the very corners of her mouth.

***

Firelight, the warmth of it turns skin golden, luminescent; faces glow, lips elbows backs and shoulders shine, shadows shape and soften. The confines of the small hide dwelling hold the light and reflect it, sharing the warm glow back and between the near white walls, funneled down onto the sleeping furs and blankets of the two, true people within. Embers glow orange and yellow, small blue flames lap and tease, and lazy small smoke barely curls as it floats up and out, smudging dark stains that collect and discolor the skins near the top.

In winter there is a stone basin to fill with rocks. Rocks heat the interior and bright lights spark when aromatic herbs hit them and flash into floating ember, the occasional orange-white star escaping outwards and upwards. And here too, on the wall around are painted stories, painted memories, and there, warm water for washing or turning into teas. All these and now, the low murmuring of lovers spent, reciting their love, retelling their love. Then a short intake of breath, a small bright gasp and an involuntary moan and the two are off, into the night-time sky, soaring amongst the stars, brilliant and clear, blue, red and yellow galaxies and the milky way like a huge cloud across the darkness. Constellations bend and crane to see these lovers fly, all creation shares in their ecstasy, rising to a hard peak then falling into bliss, soft as a sigh.

A sigh as soft as the light, as the shadow and the smoke, a sigh soft as the touch of wonder and questioning and knowing, and sometimes they sleep and even then, they cannot tell nor say who is who, which is which.

***

As the sky begins to lighten and the birds wake and call, the two open their eyes and gaze into one another and meet in such a way that across any distance, across any time, they will know one another, always. Quick and easy laughter as sweet as the stirring bird's songs and they tussle a bit and push and pull, moving with the easy energy of wild things, wild creatures, and finally he is more out of the blankets than in and so rises and stares down and he cannot be stern, he cannot be somber in the face of such profound happiness. And for a moment he turns away so that she does not see the almost tear, the absolute full complete finished that is his love for her, because then where is left to go? And he sweeps out of the shelter and into the morning cold where a mist hangs over the grasses and the waters, and the horse steams with each breath and stamps to stay warm.

With a loud WHOOP! Young Warrior lopes to the water's edge and straight away in and the stinging is immediate and hot on the skin, and he shouts and slaps himself and jumps up and down dancing from foot to foot, deeper and deeper until he can plunge into a shallow dive. The woman inside has been holding her breath and her laughter until she knows he is head under and then she stands letting blankets fall and pads out into the cold, cool grasses and looks out to the water, waiting for the man's head to rise, to break above the mirror, the mist, the water warmer than the surrounding air which is not to say that it is warm at all.

And while Young Warrior snorts and shouts and splutters and splashes, Woman walks down to the water and in. Her feet slip into the river, the stream, so smoothly that no ripple betrays or announces her presence. It is that way when one does not intrude. This is the way of the natural person. Walking deeper she pulls the soft broad leaves to use as a rag and washes her skin and soaps her hair the old way, with the old plants, the way it was for her mother and all mothers as far back as anyone knows, and she pretends to not see the man stealthing toward her, slipping through the water like serpent or fish. But when he arrives, she is gone, has moved up on the bank, wringing her hair dry, shaking it this way and that, and just the way her body moves leaves the man stunned and still and mouth hanging open breathless and mute. The woman tosses a look over her shoulder as she laughs her way back to shelter and clothing and cooking and eating and the work which is not work but life itself.

The young man smiles, and he does not think why, there is no interpretation necessary, smiles just are, faces just are and it seems there is no thickness, no space between feeling, heart, expression, step. He calls out to Horse who comes for a rub. And so, begins the everyday, the average day, the only day of note.

Horror

It is hard to say what warps some men.

The tired, grey horse noses his way down slope, stepping soft, hooves missing the dry snapping sticks and the round rolling stone. He moves slow and breathes easy. This horse knows that the man on his back is not asleep, but you wouldn't have, had you seen him.

The Old Man sits straight and easy, his legs dangle, arms hang loose, and hands rest on his thighs. Old Man's eyes are closed but not squeezed, only resting soft as in repose. The valley creatures circle warily round horse and man, there is no overt threat, but something, some unnatural stillness is there surrounding them, surrounding the man. The cold, hollow space they make moves, and the animals are confused.

Old Man is a murderer, but so at ease with his conscience that he gives off no conflicting signal, only quiet. He winds and wends his secret, deadly way. The old man and his horse with their unnatural quiet, move as mist and fog, sinking heavy and soft, down, down, into the valley. Still, the young man warrior and the woman would have known...

But they are so happy, their intention is turned. The couple's awareness is pointed wholly towards one another with none left over for the valley floor.

The old man's horse stops and settles. Old Man raises his head, eyes still closed he inhales then sighs without a sound. Slowly his eyes open and he reads the signs, he intuits or feels the two true people and the couple's horse, who perks up his ears and stamps in nervous detection. For a moment, the pregnant Woman straightens and peers out towards the wood but, she does not quite see the terrible Old Man, only shadow. And now the animals understand, and they go still and move to their own hiding spots already knowing death comes here. It seems to them that every human story has tragedy.

Slowly the strange Old Man turns away from the two and the horse and the camp. And his horse climbs up the hill in the same noiseless way he descended. The old man's back is towards the camp, but his attention is on the valley none the less.

And in the valley below, the blissful.

The Young Warrior has pulled a fish trap from the stream, it is built of willow branches and they are bent and curved. The trap has collected a meal sized trout who still does not know that this is her very last day and that she is irrevocably caught, trapped, because in her animal innocence, she has swum into a cage that has no way out. The good, Young Warrior is hoisting the trap made of branches onto the bank and the water is streaming off the branches, they are shiny from it, wet and dark, and the trout is flip-flopping but not terribly so. The brilliant colors of the silvery fish, the black spots and the golden hue, the cage settling down onto the soft, thick green grass that grows near the bank, all reek of life and newness and morning and beginning. The Young Warrior pauses and is still. His face is not moving, his gaze is turned inward, until suddenly he starts, turns his attention outward and spins to look towards the woman and stare.

She is there, bent over at work on some project, some story, some artifact, something to hold a new human, a tiny thing tight against her body. A faint smile on her lips, her brow is furrowed in concentration and her hair is hanging down, hiding part of her face and the Young Warrior takes a small hesitant step in her direction and she looks up and he knows. He sees it and is certain of it and the knowledge hits him and fills him and swells him to bursting and the woman stands and drops her carrier and faces the young man and turns her arms so that they are held slightly away from her body and her palms are facing the young warrior and she is proud and fierce and more powerful than any force the young warrior has ever seen, glowing with the life that grows inside her.

He slow walks, trots, then runs to her and now afraid to touch her; slowing, stopping, suddenly afraid that he might harm her, but she is laughing and leaps into his arms and presses her wet cheek against his and holds on and says it is okay until he wraps his arms around her, gently first, then stronger and something is welling up in his throat and it is a joyous shout and he is spinning and spinning so fast that the woman's legs are twirling out as they turn. He stops and gently sets her down on her feet and she is on tip toe and smiling, shining and she nods *yes*. And now the young warrior runs a few feet and turns and questions and races back. It is an entire conversation of questions and answers and resolution and doubt, love and then fear and pride until finally, the woman reaches out and touches him and stops him and stills him.

They will have a child.

***

The dark, strange Old Man up the hill, feels a welling up. Some shiver, some thrill of energy races up and along his spine, life and purpose begin to fill his arms and legs and Horse feels the expansion and bleak black power and his head comes up a bit, held higher with purpose.

Old Man on other side of the hill, dismounts, and his horse begins to snuffle and pull at the grass and move slowly away. Old Man's horse has witnessed this strange routine before. It is the changing.

The Old Man makes an offering to the earth and the sky and one to the wind, he would smoke on it, but the smell might give him away. And he strips down, until yes, his only clothing is a loin cloth and strips of buckskin wound tight around his arms and just above his knees. He will use these to staunch the flow of blood should his prey wound him in an extremity. And Old Man is now Bad Man, and he is slick with grease, and he holds the knife, the club and the bow low down by his thigh and there are three arrows in his bow hand. He has tied back his white hair and uses ashes saved from the three days ago fire to cover his face, he has carried these ashes and saved this fat for this moment, and he applies it to himself, and he becomes indistinct and hard to tell from the greys of some tree trunks and the shadows of leaf and branch. His breathing is slow and deep and there is no rush in him, no ringing in his ears, only a sense that he is acting according to his being, he is moving as is his purpose. Stepping left, then right and easing himself into the nature, turning his thoughts to stillness, tuning his breath to the swirling wind and stepping when leaves rustle, when wind blows and he is swimming through the forest, the air thick as water, carrying information as water carries flotsam, pulsing and eddying here and there and he moves in the creases, never standing out and even the birds are startled into silence when they notice him, if they notice him, and he is there and watching the young warrior with the fish. And the arrow in his hand is nocked in the bow and released. Flying, it strikes the young warrior deep. The dive and roll and breaking the arrow shaft off and the Bad Man is sprinting, impossibly fast. And the warrior has forgotten that a moment ago he was dreaming of his child and now, he is fully engaged, fully involved but so far behind, too far behind and the clubbing, stabbing Bad Man has struck him down and is running, stooping down on his true prey, the woman. He intends to murder her.

Woman has seen her man go down and instead of fleeing is charging the Bad Man and it is so unusual that he is puzzled long enough, and she stabs deep, through his ribs and into his heart and the strange Bad Man is dead on his feet. Woman is swinging again, stabbing his neck and driving him back and down and still he shows nothing, no look of shock, no asking, no telling, nothing but evil. As Bad Man is ending, as he is leaving, he perpetrates one last act of murder. He slashes low on Woman's abdomen and she is gutted, her blood falls so deep red, so urgent, that she is down, unconscious. And the hateful ghost stabs once more as he leaves this place and begins his journey to hell.

Horse has launched himself towards Woman and Warrior and death. He arrives to find the Bad Man dead, the Woman unconscious and the young warrior bleeding and staggering towards the woman. And the young man falls to his knees and tries putting every piece back and the Woman cries out and regains awareness. And the horror of it, the all of it is flashing fleeting in her eyes and she knows, she knows, and she reaches for the young man. This last thing, this last moment she holds him tight and seeks to stop HIS bleeding, but he is screaming plummeting into the void and so, she calms him with her touch and searches his eyes and tells him once more,

WE

And she fades and is gone.

The young man wails aloud and even Raven knows to keep quiet. He turns his head and averts his eyes and in the almost silence, even the stream's song seems low and mournful. Horse nudges the young warrior, watches him collapse onto his side, then roll to his back. For the young warrior, the world is only black and dark and cold and empty.

SWEAT

Pain

There really isn't room for anything else. The young warrior doesn't feel pain, he IS pain. It is all he knows and all there is, morning, sunrise, evening, sunset, burning, piercing, cutting, all-consuming pain like an orange consciousness, a yellow brightness, filling the all of him. Whether his eyes are open or closed does not matter. There is only this pain.

The warrior does not mind or resist or even wish for relief, he lives here. And in some corner of his pain lit mind, Warrior understands that should he escape these bodily sensations, his pain would increase, grow worse. And the warrior, he knows how to handle pain, he is no stranger to hurt, but the end, the quit, the nothing left inside, is new to him. And if the young warrior is allowed to follow this ending path, this quitting way, unmolested, his heart will actually stop beating. The instinct to live has left him, and like the old ones who sit down and accept death and refuse food or drink and do not suffer anymore only fade into the great beyond and become one with the stars and the galaxies and the all, he has accepted this change.

This is how she finds him; this is how she knows him.

Medicine Woman sees.

***

And so, the Medicine Woman ties him, lashes him to stakes and binds him so that he cannot move. She side-steps his acceptance of the pain, his acceptance of death and convinces his body that he is bound and controlled and captive and held and some remote place in his nervous system cannot abide this captivity and so he struggles to escape the woven strands of hide and does not consider that this, this struggle, is itself a sign of life.

Medicine Woman does not take it as a good sign or bad, it only is what is. The warrior's body will survive.

She has tricked him into living, and he will not wake grateful.

*　*　*

While Warrior thrashes and struggles in wounded sleep, Medicine Woman drums and sings and glows from the inside. There is some fire inside her. She, in many ways, is as a campfire in the wild darkness, a beacon that calls the wicked and the wonderful alike. Some come seeking warmth and companionship and some small sustenance, some come to see what they might take. She is a campfire. Her hands are warm; her face is immutable, unchanging, timeless. She is only what is needed.

Medicine Woman sits and drums and sings. The fire flares with each gust of wind, and settles with the stillness, and the woman is that, just the same, only it is in her most still moments that her flames rise near to her surface and her eyes seem to shine and her skin seems to glow.

Medicine Woman pours the healing liquid. It sits in the crease of the Young Warrior's lips, shimmering silver, tiny dark globes, building weight, pooling, until finally, spluttering and sipping and coughing, he swallows. The young warrior does not know if he resists the potion or if he is just too gone to remember how to drink.

Medicine Woman sings and hums and the firelight defines the size of the world as it expands and contracts. It is a perfect circle of light. And so, it seems there is constant contest, the darkness wants in, the Medicine Woman says no, and fuel burns. There is very little smoke. More drumming, more singing, more liquids. Retie the strips of hide, hammer the stakes in deeper, and the young warrior pulls and thrashes and moans and slowly after many hours, after some days, his moans become protestations and he wrests one arm free, days later two.

Medicine Woman knows that soon he will free himself and then what?

***

Warrior rejoins this world, born as a long keening wail. Heartache and desolation merge and mix and weave his thick blanket made of mourning and pain. There is nothing, nothing left save hurt.

And the Medicine Woman watches. It cannot be said that she is merciless, but she is unmoved. The young warrior is not attempting escape outward anymore, instead he is turning inward, and in these moments, madness is the kindest experience to allow. She will wait, watch and see. Let his madness come and deliver its relief, wisdoms and visions.

The raven and the vultures come and slap-slap with their dark feathered wings, battering the wounded. They beat Young Warrior with here, with now, demanding he return and inhabit this body. Swirling memories of his wife fill his mind like smoke, like hallucinations and as the madness gives way to weeping, sobbing, body quaking sorrows flooding and filling every seam and crevasse until there is no escape inside and the tears stream down his face as rivers to an ocean and at last Woman turns and goes back among her tasks, knowing that his pain is only just beginning, and that the warrior is going to live.

Darkness. Why darkness?

For a moment after he opens his eyes he is confused. Then he remembers that this is night, and that there, those are stars and that the smell of smoke and fire.

Woman places a bowl in his hands, some fragrance he is not familiar with fills his nostrils. He is not hungry yet, but she gently lifts his hands towards his mouth and helpless he drinks rather than drown and the taste is bitter and strange.

The liquid fills his mouth and overflowing runs down his chin, changing as it goes into fire, serpent liquid gold and heat and he starts, knowing the Woman has poisoned him and still not feeling, only wondering at the strange happenings taking place. The golden liquid fire is steaming and coalescing into some solid, some orange red phoenix rising bird beast creature spreading its wings and suddenly it is shattered by some dark straight pointed weight which pierces and fractures this vision into shards of brilliant temporary light which fall to the ground and wink into darkness, just as embers away from the flame cool and disappear.

As the light inside him grows dim, melancholy rises as a sad bear, a certain and distinct flavor of madness. And the bear begins to chew, to consume, to devour life. The bear is eating moments and days and decades, and the Woman is there in the meadow with the bear, and she strikes hard with her fist, straight into his nose and the bear rears up on hind legs and is become a raging thing, an angry beyond animal thing and it is him, the young man warrior. The bear has become the young warrior, face a rictus, a mask of hatred. As the young warrior witnesses his face shift and crack and become the face of the man who stole his whole everything, he is screaming, screaming and writhing on the ground and Medicine Woman only watches. Some tearing, some horror of ripping and there is the young warrior emerging, birthing from the Bad Man's flesh and clawing himself out gruesome and slick. Warrior is vomiting the poison from his body and it is black, like coal, like the rock that burns. He had seen coal once, brought from some far-away place as a sort of magic. The smell made him cough and gag and he had turned from it then as he turns from this now and then he is seeing the fire and the Medicine Woman sitting, watching, face lit and glowing by the flame between them. And a resignation comes as the young warrior realizes that he will not die. He slumps and is small and cries quietly. And the medicine woman begins to sing low, and her words are older than memory and carry power.

Warrior does not know, the number of hours, the number of nights. He only knows that finally a sunrise comes, and he raises his head and gazes to the Woman. There is some exchange, some conversation and he tries to stand. The Woman reaches and begins to drum, and the Young Warrior hears the faraway flute and rises to his feet. Turning with questions,

Where is the flute? I cannot see.

He cannot see from whence the notes float in, and the Woman smiles and stands, and before his very eyes she is shifting and changing and becoming and now an enormous, golden elk stands in front of the Young Warrior and encourages him to climb onto his back and the young man staggers to the elk and reaches out as in a dream to touch, tentative. The dark, thick, golden fur feels like life in his stroking, grasping hand and he shakes his head. He will not ride this animal.

The giant beast moves irresistible as time.

The meadow is silver but not of the shiny sort, the grasses are soft not brittle, and Young Warrior is pulled forward and up, up slope.

Where?

Where does this song start?

Is this my father's father?

And the Great Golden Elk tosses his head and with a flick of antlers lifts the young man onto his back and now they move fast.

Do elk fly?

It seems so as they move over entire ages and through vast ever green forests and skim alongside a grey lichen-streaked cliff. The haunting flute plays on and the drum still insists, and the young man warrior is unable to stay soft and so unseats himself and falls, rises to his feet and is running to the edge of the cliff and staring over. There below is a small village, a dog, a fire, a home and a man. The man there plays the flute so beautifully that the young warrior grows tears, and they fill his eyes. The song is a medicine and pain is weeping out of Young Man as tears and where they fall on the pine needle ground, flowers erupt in brilliant color and soft waving forgiveness and the young man warrior collapses to his knees.

The elk moves off, moves away. The young man starts and stares up at the elk. He feels.

Loss. There is loss and leaving, losing and changing.

Elk gazes back at the warrior,

Life is change, and loss holds a beauty all its own, same as love.

And Elk's brown eyes shine with warmth and the Young Warrior only sobs.

Warrior opens his eyes; Medicine Woman sits still and quiet. She is a mountain, a tree, a shelter and wind and the young man understands where he is and what is happening.

Raven glides down and settles on the Woman's shoulder. She stands and moves to the lodge's entrance. Just before she sweeps the blanket out of the doorway, she points to a lake.

Wash.

Medicine Woman disappears into her lodge and Young Man stands. His legs tremble; weak, he stumbles forward to the lake he has never in all his travels seen. His feet feel the cold wet bank, soft and alive and green. He sees the great legged frog poised to leap and swim and yet the young man still cannot find joy. Still, he staggers farther out into the water, ankle deep, then shin deep and the line where water meets air meets skin feels like a burning above and numb below. Deeper still, knees then waist and sinking submerging exhaling down into the liquid, feeling the knife edge surface line move up his skin and close over his head.

He stays there, under the surface, for some moments listening to the lake. What can Lake say to him? And faint, there is a gurgling, a bubbling sound of water rising from deep...up through the rocks and sand, filling the small lake and Water says that she is from the earth and so she nourishes all the peoples and cleanses those who wash in this way and then she will rise into the sky and watch down and fall down to the earth and go back deep. A lake, like a day, like a life, a circle.

Rising, surfacing and an inhale, an inspiration and the life goes into him and fills his lungs and it is not easy, life. It is cold sometimes and can burn and there is fear and pain and love and yes loss and the Young Warrior is not so young. Breath moves in and breath moves out, like a day, like a night, like a life.

The warrior stands there still as stone and watches as the water quiets, the ripples fall and flatten, and the mirror surface reflects. He is only breathing, experiencing the beating in his chest as it fits into the expanding and contracting, and this rhythmic rise and fall fascinates him, and he is only present to the lake. This moment, this gift captures him and holds his attention. The no longer young man only raises his eyes when a great heron skims in for a landing and at the last minute makes a sparkling splash. The magnificent bird, startled by the human's presence, is clumsy.

**

In the morning, in the mist, dew drops sit atop blades of grass and split the light, sparking here and there like jewels, like gems, but so short lived that only the attentive ever own them and then, sometimes, even the awakened forget and do not see.

Medicine Woman notices these things. She sees the birds asleep and the sky greying up as the night time darkness flees from the light of the rousing sun. Her hair is long and thick, streaked with grey or silver and her skin is brown like pine needles. She stands and raises her arms to the rising sun and the birds sing good mornings and she is a conductor of sorts by virtue of her there-ness, her awareness, her connection to that deep underneath vibration frequency rumble of waves that pass through all.

The softest of breezes kisses her cheek and greets her awakening and she is softly moving as if blown by the gentle wind down to the water's edge. There she pauses to remove her dress. The dress, no matter how soft, is too much sometimes, too much distance between her and now, her and here and once bare she moves to wade into the lake.

Her hands skim just above the surface and though they do not touch the water, waves propagate outwards as if announcing their happiness at her arrival. Water welcomes her as friend, as family, as elemental and the fish dance and dart around her legs and Medicine Woman smiles and warmth returns. Willows, ferns, all bend towards her to drink of this strange light that emanates shines forth. This is not a loud thing. These moments are not so unusual as to elicit remark from those that are there. I only articulate them here so that you, never having been privy to her presence can understand something of her nature. Medicine Woman does not make a show of praying. It's routine, no less beautiful for the regularity, but essentially her norm.

The Man is wakened by the birds' songs and he rubs the sleep from his eyes and the salt from his face and presses himself upright and searches out, his eyes moving from close to far and round the compass and seeing Medicine Woman standing in the lake he gasps. Her shape is Woman, the very essence archetype of female nurture, lush, rich, compassion and strength, of depth, of water, of calm and storm. Her skin is covered with permanent lines and he sees her there as a moon, as the moon, silver white shining glowing and pulling tidal waters towards herself and then letting them fall. There is no particular hush around her, instead, there is some environmental sigh of contentment as even the air seems to move softly outwards in waves, in plumes, in swirls and universal shapes of power when she moves her hands. And she sings and chants and mountains move, clouds come and go, trees sprout, become saplings and go skyward, reaching their arms high and wide to shelter, to worship to touch the sky to commune with God.

As the Man Warrior rises from his blankets and stands full of wonder and awe, she turns and looks to him, sees into him and fills up his eyes.

The medicine woman leads the young warrior to a small clearing that is some 40 feet removed from the lake's edge. This ground is a bit unusual in that it is soft and dry and sweet grasses carpet the ground. Rocks are everywhere in this land, but this one spot seems somehow barren of stone, perhaps long ago someone policed the area and left it this way, soft as a carpet.

Medicine Woman draws a circle on the ground and hands the young man a stick.

Dig a hole as big around as this stick is long. This notch here, measures the depth.

The Warrior Man is weak and emotionally spent. Still, he begins to search about for a tool to make the digging easier. At last, he drops to his knees and scratches out the dimensions on the surface of the earth and begins digging. Medicine Woman, seeing the young warrior punching the sharp stick into the dirt, loosening handfuls and then raking those handfuls out, is satisfied. She turns and leaves to walk and commune with the nature around.

The young warrior digs a foot down and three feet round, leveling the dirt and the space around. Medicine Woman is walking and marking fallen trees. When the hole is dug the young warrior lines the bottom and sides with flat stone, taking care to fit them tightly. There is no hurry. Each stone has a place and a reason and a voice. Soon there is a rock lined pit in the earth surrounded by flat dirt. As the young man finishes constructing the pit, Woman points to the saplings she has marked. Young man collects the fallen and the felled and brings them to Medicine Woman. Together they begin construction of a low small structure. The shell is made of lashed together saplings. It would barely hold four people. There are fours and windows to the sky and each branches placement, each and every knot and binding holds meaning and purpose. Medicine Woman's hands move in certainty and her instruction is simple and straight. Her mother has taught her well. Next, Medicine Woman shows the young warrior how to shape and fashion large mud bricks and stack them in a circular shape, until a small low dome is finished and sits drying in the sun.

The doorway faces east, is low, and to enter you must crawl and duck your head. There are skins and blankets which drape to cover the entry and when they are closed it is darker than night inside. A short walk away is a large fire pit with flat stones set in a large square. Next to the fireplace the young warrior and the medicine woman begin stacking tree fall, branches and small trees which have succumbed to wind or erosion or just overcrowding.

Medicine Woman motions to the young warrior and directs him to go and collect rocks, and she does not show him the size or shape or type. Warrior Man, still weak and empty, stumbles out and away and begins to collect rocks one at a time bringing them back to the fireplace and Medicine Woman, who sits on a large smooth rock and is grinding some flower, some herb, some root into fine particles and storing the fragrant powders in small animal skin bags with thong ties and colorful decorations painted and sewn onto their sides. She nods her head,

Yes.

And so, she instructs Young Warrior in the construction of the sacred fire.

The way it goes is a layer of wood and a layer of rock and a layer of wood and so on until there is a pyre? A bonfire, a pyramid of wood and stone set and ready to burn when given spark.

And now the young man gathers water in buckets, some are made from skins and organ tissue and held open by willow ribs bent in circles, some are bladder which stretch, and fill and the skin allows just enough water to evaporate that the water is kept cool even on warm days. Some are just buckets, like any old bucket and where they come from is a mystery.

 When the woman is satisfied, she brings out a drum and passes it to the young man and bids him play. She raises her hands and her eyes and her heart to the four directions, the six directions and chants poems in a language only she and long-gone others recognize.

 I admit that I harbor the idea that some animals understand these words because they gather and sit and watch the woman and the young man as he drums. And the animals look on with approval and equanimity and occasionally respond and echo back Medicine Woman's words and it is a call and call back sing song chanting, and the drumbeat collects them all in its rhythm and beat and hollow vibrating sound.

The fire is lit, and it is a huge fire, with heat radiating out so that you cannot stand anywhere near it. The grasses are singed and burnt back in a circle. And the animals' eyes glow even in the early evening sun light as they patrol around and around the low land which surrounds the small highland lake. They watch the humans to remind them, to make certain they do not forget again or ever, that we all live here, breathe here, find our way home here. And the young warrior drums and Medicine Woman chants and as the sun sets so do the highest flames and there are embers glowing white hot and stones amongst them and Medicine Woman is ready, and the young warrior is still without his own intention and so will move as a ghost wherever she asks.

Medicine Woman uses a stick from the edge of the big fire to light the sage. Waving an eagle's wing over it she sets the purifying smoke awhirl. It is a simple ceremony, to cleanse oneself before entering the low dome, womb, lodge. To clean one's body and heart and tongue and mind and walk round the big stone and she waits and leads the young warrior through the cleansing with smoke and then explains what he should do next.

Medicine Woman goes down to her hands and knees and enters through the small opening and crawls around the stone pit and takes her place. Young Warrior uses a long sapling to drag a stone out of the glowing pile of embers. It is so hot there that the sapling end bursts into flame, but it was cut green and won't burn once out of the heat.

The young man drags, lifts the stone and delivers it into the lodge, setting it down carefully in the center of the round stone pit. Woman taps sharply on the stone with her own hook shaped piece of wood or bone. It is difficult to say what the tool is, so old and decorated with carvings and burned spots. But she taps to seat the rock and to crack it if it has the desire to open. Six more times young man repeats this exercise half dragging, half carrying the stone into the lodge and each time the Woman taps and positions and points and instructs, she follows some instinct some knowing older than history and when the seventh stone is in place, she bids the young man enter.

He stoops, and it is not low enough, so he goes to hands and knees and then fully prone to crawl into this dark, hot, place. There is very little light, only what leaks through the space around his body and through the low entry.

To the south.

She points, and he is careful to crawl left and careful where he places his hands and feet and knees and elbows. The stones glow orange with heat and already he is sweating heavily. At last, he is seated upright, and the crown of his head is brushing the ceiling and the air is so hot that to breathe is difficult.

Medicine Woman gazes at him steadily as she plays the drum low, barely tapping its taut skin and the sound fills the small space and she nods, and the young warrior lets the door covering fall closed.

Remember

Darkness comes so complete that he cannot see the medicine woman or the walls or the doorway,

What if it has disappeared! What if there is no more doorway, no portal, no return and no way back?

And the beginnings of a panic come to him, and this is good because fear means he wants to live. And then he can see the glowing orange and red of the stones, the ancestors, those who have been here so long, before man, before animal, before thought.

Medicine Woman throws a pinch of some herb, some leaf, some sap and there is a white light on the stone so brilliant it is as a doorway to another dimension, an opening into the original place, the original world of light. And then she is drumming more insistently and as the vibrations and the heat and the darkness and the low ceiling rob the young warrior of reference point, of touchstone, he begins to look only to the glowing stones. The orange light reflects in his eyes and there is only that thin thread of connection to this time, this place and the drum is creating waves in the line of connection and light until there is only this original place, this original time, this original world.

Medicine Woman begins to intone, I am, My mother was, my father and grandfather and his father and stretching backing into the mist of early times she recounts her place, her name and her ancestors and knowing this river stretches out farther than time can be measured, generation after generation, this gives a place, a solidity, that cannot be blown away like dust in the wind. This stream of connecting peoples and histories gives root and strength that cannot be erased. Medicine Woman is part of the eternal, a single note in a symphony and she has peace. The young warrior sits silent.

He cannot name, he does not name, he does not remember and so is adrift, afloat, untethered in this big universe and thus he is thrown this way and that as any whim or breeze. If he has any roots at all they lie in his grief, his memory of violence done, and love leaked out onto the good earth as rusty thick water and gone. And in this silence Medicine Woman sings louder.

Her voice is the story, is the cry of all the people before her, don't forget, don't get lost. And as she sings and drums the walls expand and push back, growing the lodge larger and larger and there are ten people here, ancestors sure. And more than ten, singing and drumming and the sounds have become deafening and there are a hundred people, and they all know the words and they all know the story and some of the people are from before and some of the people are from next and so there you have in the one time, the one people and the one sweat and one song and drum.

Young Warrior is drunk, intoxicated on the connection, on the belonging, secure for this moment, no death, no birth only forever now. All the peoples are here. And Medicine Woman cracks hard on the drum and the pulsing stops and the singing stops. More herbs thrown on the stone and white, yellow orange red lines streak across the surface of the stones and began to talk and tell. Here is how we began, here is how we went, here is where we fall. And greed is shown and how even the ones who kill the most, own the most are not content but troubled and restless and always fearing that what they have is not enough.

Young Warrior sees this. This is no hallucination. The stones, they speak and crack and draw and show and the young man is riveted by the tale. Medicine Woman sits with eyes on the stones, she knows this story from a thousand times and knows her part and feels... still. Only the stirrings of time travel trickle, like a tiny stream snaking thin through her awareness. And then she pours the herbal waters onto the stones and a great hissing so loud as to hurt the ears goes and the heat is so intense the young warrior fears he will die. He lowers his face as near the floor as possible and smells the dirt, the earth, the cool cleanliness and he breathes deep of this earth and understands that he is from this earth and will return to this earth and now he is knowing his first mother and his first father, and finally, he is hearing his family's names. The low intimate rolling under sound of them starts a whisper in his heart, his brain, his inside ear and grows and spreads through his body as fog fills a valley, filling all of the cracks and crannies and leaving him more solid, more still, more full than before. Tears of shame stream down his face. Sorrow for his forgetfulness, but it is not too late. And he knows that it is not too late and so he sits, back straight, head lifted high into the heat of the low mud roof, which now, empty of all but himself and Medicine Woman, seems much larger than the place he had crawled into some time before.

Medicine Woman taps the young warrior's thigh, and he folds himself to the side and pushes aside the door cover. Cool, early evening air swirls in feline like, rubbing herself against the young warrior and the medicine woman, insinuating down into their lungs and their visions are carried up and fill the low dome lodge and then out into the evening and up towards the heavens. The Young Warrior shivers.

DOOR

Medicine Woman closes her eyes and hums, a small smile on her face. Young Warrior scrubs the salt off his face with his palms and blinks and looks around to see where all the peoples have gone. Medicine Woman sighs and points with her stick and the young man crawls out of the lodge and rolling onto his back looks up at the early night-time sky. Stars are everywhere, there are no blank, dark places in the sky.

It's funny how different everything looks. The young warrior does not smile, but some complete sort of sigh, marks some slight shift and he is thirsty. He knee-walks over to the water bladder and drinks. A small splash on his feverish face and a sip and all the nations are watching, and he sees their eyes glowing and hears their padding footfalls.

Medicine Woman taps the drum in quick successive beats and gestures. Seven more stones. And Young Warrior retrieves his sapling with the blackened, forked end and begins to bring the stones from the bonfire remains into the lodge. And Medicine

Woman sits straight and breathing steady, and she is as implacable as time, loving but final and stern.

The stones are set, and Young Warrior beckoned, crawls back inside the low, soft, lodge and the dirt is cool on his hands and feet, but the air is hot and promises pain. Pain enough to drive him back inside himself, through those places where he believes he is stuck and deeper still into something, some place beyond himself, back to the place where all of him lives at once. The original place. The place of Ancestors and descendants and the big story.

The woman taps his thigh, and he lets fall the covering and all is dark again, save for the deep burning orange of the stones in their place.

SWEAT

The Young Warrior sits, and Medicine Woman begins the drumming. Low, slower, earth instead of fire, and the heat is filling up the tiny space and the heat seems liquid and the young warrior is immersed and under and he feels the heat pressing against his nostrils and eyes and seeking entry and for long moments he resists and holds, but the heat is incessant and insistent and soon he is breathing it down deep inside, filling his lungs and there it is leaking out into his blood and being carried along to every space inside himself and he is becoming the heat.

Darkness has a weight, like a blanket, and it is pushing him, pressing the Young Warrior down towards the earth and Medicine Woman is singing softly. He waits for the small lodge to expand, to fill with people as before but this time there is no expanding and no more peoples and even the medicine woman's voice is softening and tapering off into emptiness. Only the low, soft beat of the drum remains, and it can easily be mistaken for a heartbeat, his heartbeat, push-pulling his strumming blood, moving it behind and through his ears and into his pulsing hands and feet. Young Warrior's fingers and toes twitch to dance but there is no song from anywhere out and so he falls, farther and farther in.

The alone-ness is overwhelming, the empty, the great void and he is floating in some vast blackness, devoid of light and sound, only his own pulsing blood and beating heart remain and he is afraid, afraid, afraid and alone and adrift and Medicine Woman pours the water, throws the water, splashes the water onto the stones and there is a cracking and the young warrior is blinded for a moment as light flashes and this is worse than before, deeper than before, because now he cannot even envision himself floating there in space, even Young Warrior's concept of self has gone dark and invisible and he is no thing, no person, no spirit, only an absence.

There is the heat, hissing steam and Woman hissing too, and some new fragrance, and the young man is sniffing, casting about, trying to identify what smell, what grass is this? This is the grass of the meadow he had shared with wife. This is the grass of Young Warrior's home and he sees the golden, silvery, soft leaves of grass and the beauty brings tears to his

56

eyes and he is trailing his hands lightly over the tips of the grass and feeling the tickle on his fingers and on the soles of his feet.

And then the wetness comes and turning his hand he sees his palm red, red like the fog that descends over his mind and blankets and blocks all things from view. It is her blood and her blood and his blood too, mixed and thick on top of the grasses, running down and soaking into the earth. It is impossible to say what holds the young warrior upright. It is his whole everything collapsed and folded inside and all he can see are his whole life gone and they are lying there and softening and returning and the young warrior wails aloud in his grief and Medicine Woman bangs the drum in time and whispers the words of grief.

The girl he loved, the girls he loved are going down into the earth and the young warrior would follow. He pushes his fingers deep into the loamy earth, and fingers and soil are merging, and he is pressing elbow deep, shoulder deep and deeper. He places his skull on the surface of dirt and pushes and he is submerging like a diver, down into the murkiness in pursuit, in longing, in joy really, following his love to the down below, the other under place and the light comes and the people come, but they are ghosts, they do not need him, the people run and play and work and he can only witness. He wails again, a loud keening cry of longing and loss and Medicine Woman sings and strikes the drum, and the young man realizes that He is the ghost and, in this place, inconsequential.

His tears make a puddle, a trickle, a stream, and a river, and it flows from before, to born, to life, to the dying death part and then beyond to the Original place again and the underneath is gone, and only stars remain.

Somehow, someway, Young Warrior is gazing up and seeing stars and millions of stars and the constellations are shapes and they smile, and he cannot smile back. He looks behind and sees the face of the Bad Man. The Bad Man, his chest torn open where the young warrior was born, and he sees there the lined and drawn and weary face and the dead eyes and the scars of torture. And turning to see the young wife, his young wife and her thick hair and ready teasing laugh and fleet feet and she is beckoning him closer and taking his hand and smiling so sweet, so gentle, and she leads him away from the red grass and towards the clear waters of the stream.

Turning the young warrior to face her and looking full upon him, she smiles and caresses his cheek and pulls him closer and smells him and touches her cheek against his chest and then gently presses him back and away. She sees her husband so sad; he is sorrow. She looks so concerned and serious and she is going in through his eyes, into his mind and down deeper into his heart and it is beating in time and there are two buh-bumps and she makes certain he understands and she makes the sign; we will meet again under this blue sky and love again under those warm blankets and then she pulls him out into the stream, into the water and he is going under feet first, the water rising deeper, deeper until his chin and then his face and Young Warrior sees his wife's love filled face go wavery as the water divides the light and then he is in the lodge, drenched in sweat and Medicine Woman is beating the drum fast and hard. He has chased his grief, followed its path down, to, through and back. And for the remainder of his, this life it will be a thread, a strand, a piece of him. And Medicine Woman sings the most melancholy song, but, down low in the scale and occasionally high there is a note, the reminder and the light.

The Young Warrior joins in the song and he does not know how he knows the words. The medicine woman knows. This song is human and temporal, and it is the song of change. All those who are born will know the words. The young warrior sings the name of his love and his would have been child and his long-lost people. And down below the red grass the people feel loved.

Medicine Woman taps the young warrior's thigh, and he falls, crawls to the entry and folds the flap back and the wash of cold night air goes over his face like some new slapping pain and it stings his eyes and puts a hitch in his breathing, and he crawls steaming out into the crystal-clear night. The stars are so near, so bright he can see the altar rock and the implements placed there and there. Crisp and oddly remote, there is a sort of unreality about it all.

FALSE DOOR

At once he is reaching and touching the water skin
and lifting and drinking deep and he knows it is not
good for his stomach, but he is thirsty, so thirsty.
And glowing eyes witness him there. A young man
on his knees, dripping water down his chin and
chest and shiny with the sheen of sweat and dark
smudges where he has pressed into the earth and
he has some strange sort of fever and some strange
sort of balance and the coyote trickster comes out
into the moon's light and the starlight and his coat
is silver and drops hang on his whiskers like jewels
and he with his laughing face and lolling tongue and
haughty tail steps dainty to the young man and
sniffs. And then two more show and three, soon a
circle and the coyote are all chattering and sniffing,
and the man is certain he is hallucinating and so he
finds none of this unusual and the Woman still sits
across from the door, peering out with glittering
eyes and a small smile, surely the coyote will have
tales to share of singing with a sick, mad man. And
soon someone stretches their throat and cries out
or laughs and somehow it all mingles into one

mournful, joyful, resonating, resounding song celebrating life and the young man has joined in and his eyes are closed as he howls up towards the night sky. Somewhere between a sob and hysteria Young Warrior sings out into the star filled sky. And then the pack is rushing off into the grass, into the wild darkness and only the young warrior is there, calling to the moon for consolation or release or at the very least companionship. And Medicine Woman thrums the drum's skin and the young warrior's head falls forward and he lays in the grass for a small moment before staggering to his feet, fetching his long, forked stick and beginning to move the next seven stones.

The contrast between the frigid night air and the blazing heat of the stones is lost on the young warrior. His fever has risen to a point where he barely notices the shimmering energy baking off the ancestors, the glowing red, the hammering drum. And when Medicine Woman pours the water onto the stones, whatever herb or root is mixed inside causes the young warrior to grow sick in his stomach. He feels it rising in his throat and the niceties must wait and he is out the door and running past the altar and into the firepit where the last stones wait and he has fallen in, stumbled face down, head down. Young Warrior dives into the pile of glowing embers and he is screaming in pain.

The burning is supposed to kill the nerves, but it does not, and Young Warrior is being consumed by the heat. The flames have leaped up with this new fuel and the place where the Bad Man's arrow penetrated is boiling and bubbling and poison is gurgling forth. Young Warrior feels it deep inside like a well, an aquifer, an underground spring and river and the black viscous liquid is pouring out and he is screaming through a throat so exhausted and raw that he is barely audible. One lone splinter left deep in the young warrior's flesh is burning and it is turned from wood to ash and the vile darkness that is flowing out of him carries the ash out and it goes into the pyre and is swallowed and lost. And the hole in Young Warrior's body is singed, cauterized, burned shut and he feels the medicine woman grasp his ankles and pull hard and he is momentarily upright, and he sees the lodge as if it is day and Medicine Woman is there, still as the altar stone, and the ancestors are glowing but silent, waiting for him to say something but he does not know what?

SWEAT

Medicine Woman hands him a rattle and she begins to thump upon the drum and Young Warrior thinks,

No, no more. I cannot. I...

And this last absurd vision goes from him, and he is seeing himself from outside his body and he thinks,

This must be death.

What is left where the young warrior sits is a skin, a barrier to rain and blood and perforated it leaks and scars, yet it breathes, and sweats and ointments pass in past skin and sweat passes out and how is this permeable THING the edge of who he is? And his memories laugh, and his dreams laugh, and the young warrior's ghost approaches and touches the skin and says MINE.

All entities present laugh uproariously at this MINE, this skin, which came from what place and where does it go when it is used up and how.

Young Warrior sees himself as from inside.

He does not want to approach this answer. But neither does he want to put it down. The new understanding is more terrible than he can hold, and yet; all that keeps him together.

There lives inside Warrior a resentment and an anger, and it is entirely justified, in fact never was a hatred more appropriate. But. There is no use for this hate that lies in his stomach coiled like a rattle snake waiting to lash out and poison whomever startles him, slips through his defenses and catching him out, surprises him.

The Bad Man is dead. The young warrior saw his corpse. Saw where he himself exited, crawled-clawed his way out of the Bad Man's chest. The Bad Man is gone and this hate, this rage, this pain is only lethal to the living. And the young warrior sees the snake in his belly coiling and turning and this snake has the features, the face of the Bad Man. He is part of the young warrior now. Lives on inside the man now, and same as a snake who lives in a cave, anyone who dares reach the Young Warrior's insides will be struck down, bitten and poisoned. And Young Warrior hates the hate and now the snakes are here, are more and more and more and he tries to stand but the ceiling is low and smacks him hard in the head and Young Warrior is back down and seated in his lonely cave surrounded by snakes, one has the face of the Bad Man and one has the face of the Young Warrior and the rest are copies and copies and infinite copies and so lose definition in the replication process until, they are all only foggy, coiling ,slithering, hate filled **things**, and the Young Warrior sits.

And, this is why Medicine Woman handed him the gourd rattle, and this is the young warrior shaking, and his warning is there,

Do not come close, do not come near,

He is a cave full of snakes. And the Young Warrior is at last satisfied, content. He sits in his poisonous cave and feels his skin dry, and wrinkles come and scars too numerous to count, and Young Warrior has visions these days and rides Horse while half asleep, only to rouse when joy comes near. The disturbing light of love is an irritant and from his cave he slithers forth and chokes the joyful simply because it hurts his eyes to see a smile and it pierces his brain when he hears a laugh, and the Young Warrior has become hard to distinguish from the Bad Man.

The ancestor stones creak and pop and the red lines and the white lines dance across their surface and Medicine Woman watches intently.

It is time. They say.

And Medicine Woman begins to drum at a different rhythm and her song has stopped and her eyes have closed, and she has gone down within and up and there she sees an entrance to a cave and smells the fear living within. Her face does not shift. Her eyes do not harden. Medicine Woman disparages stick or stone, needing neither torch nor blade. She moves on instead with intelligent feet, gliding to and through the cave's mouth and there inside is the young warrior surrounded by his snakes. He has become hard to look at. Young Warrior wears the marks left by his terrible moments and hate is in his spine and his hair and his mouth.

Medicine Woman walks forward and into and down.

***

The snakes rattle and warn and throw their strikes and drops of venom sprout on their fangs.

Medicine Woman, the Young Warrior does not know how; she sees the venom and then, the drops; they fly and fall, wet and powerless to be turned by the ground, eaten, consumed and made wholesome. The young warrior's snakes shrink; their rattles fall away. And she moves to the young warrior and takes a fist full of his hair and forcefully pulls him forward onto his face, and now she sings strong, powerful, loud.

The Young Warrior is awake, and he sees Medicine Woman there in his cave. He is baffled by the how. How has she has moved past his protectors, his defenses, his wall. And he is filled with some fear and so lashes out with the snake from his mouth and the snake from his spine, and their fangs bite deep into medicine Woman and she turns pale and ashen and grey and wavers but does not fall.

Shifting and changing in the poisonous dark, Woman has become after all, his love, his wife.

Standing there in his cave he did carve from stone and fill with venom. It is Wife! And the young warrior in his hurt has struck her down and she is falling, falling, wafting to the earthen floor like a leaf and the Young Warrior is falling and he is catching her and holding her, and her face is going but still she is smiling. And she gives the sign. I will see you under this sky again sometime and as she fades, the glowing stones brighten, they are joined in warmth, in white light deep within the igneous crust and the Medicine Woman is singing and the young warrior is shaken and grasping for his love and holding only the eyes of the Medicine Woman who drums. And he sees the rattle in his hand and casts it aside, throws it so hard that it smashes on the red rocks and breaking into shards, ignites and burns. The foul smell of the bitter root fills the lodge and the Young Warrior quick, reaches to Medicine Woman. Is she hurt? Will she die?

And Medicine Woman only sits, still again, and points at the burning rattle pieces and Young Warrior watches until they are consumed and gone.

Medicine Woman pours the water and a different herb, and the steam fills the lodge, and it does not choke the young man, only forces him low to breathe, and the clean dirt earth is sweet smelling and Woman taps his thigh and he moves to the flap.

Mother

Buffalo Man

A girl child sits, huddled next to a tree. She is wrapped in blankets and skins, still she is shaking. A heavy snow has fallen. Sounds are dull and faint, unless it is the sharp cracking break of a tree limb surrendering to the weight of the snow.

Where the young girl sits, she is surrounded by drift, icy white death only inches from her body. Overhead, snow laden branches form a dangerous roof, one waiting to collapse with a muffled crump. Heat from the girl's tiny body holds back the creeping white shroud of snow and has created a small half shelter. Her breath fogs and freezes. She is waiting to be found.

***

There is a man; he wears the skin of a buffalo. His face is smoked and deeply wrinkled and furrowed and he appears as an apparition just away from the tree. He stands with his robe folded close around. He is watching intently, not speaking. The little girl stares back. Her shaking has stopped, and she is not afraid. And so, she leans forward, and crouch walks out from under the tree and stands and there is only a great buffalo, huge and steaming and head swinging low with the weight of it. She presses forward and tangles her hands in the coarse curly fur and climbs what seems like forever until she sits tall on his back. Her red chapped hands are warmer, and she feels so tired and how can she possibly stay awake? And as she leans forward and collapses onto the giant beast's warm shoulder, she sleeps, and the great beast moves.

Buffalo

In the morning, the sun warms the child's back. Heat from the great beast warms her front and the low rumble of his breath and heartbeat, the slow swaying movement of his steps, all compose a lulling, calming experience. The grasses smell sweet and crackling dry. The beast has happily rejoined his herd and the tiny girl is surrounded by a hundred thousand lowing buffalo. Massive and largely gentle, the herd moves, dark, high plains drifters, grazing their way across the landscape like rain heavy clouds moving across the winter sky. The tiny girl is hungry and thirsty.

She sits up and her giant friend stops moving. She pulls and tugs on his curly coat and scratches his neck and hums low affectionate attaching words, then climbs down to the ground and stands, holding tightly to the giant's leg. Casting about she sees the herd and feels its warmth and she feels safe, protected.

Walking slowly next to her savior animal, she smells the herd. It is a clean sort of grassy, musky, cold wind smell that is deeply comforting. The tiny girl moves amongst the herd slow and easy, working her way to the edge. There she sees the small stream which borders the flat where the herd is shifting, shuffling, grazing. Next to its waters she kneels and peers down. The water is clear and see through and there is a delicate shelf of ice at its very edge. A white crystalline, spider-web frost, like lace, decorates the skin of dark mud. In the water she sees movement and it is golden and silver and swift. She leans forward eyes wide and watches. There among the pebbles and rocks strewn across the stream's bed, she sees crawfish, red and blue and brown and waving their claws and walking carefully along the bottom. There are greens, mosses and tiny leaved plants that sway side to side in the current and they seem a tiny sun themselves, not in color of course, but in some light or radiation or promise. The small girl dips her hands into the water, watching as the surface line creates a slanting optical effect; and she wiggles her fingers to see them move. She considers her hands, small, soft, and dexterous. She can grasp and hold and let things go, too. She flattens her hand and feels it dance with the current, slicing this way and that like a bird moving through the sky. And she wonders if the air is like the water, liquid and with currents and ebbs and flows, eddies, and swirls. Looking up, she sees the great black vulture spiraling in the wide, blue sky, barely flapping his wings, lazy and lifting higher, ever higher and surveying the land below. On impulse she waves one hand, and the vulture dips a wing in acknowledgement.

Girl cups her hands and drinks. The water is cold and thrilling and filled with goodness and the smell of earth. She leans back and sips the air, tasting its flavor and feeling it, like water with less weight, kissing her skin and swirling away as she wiggles her fingers, and she laughs.

The sound is like magic and tiny fresh flowers turn to watch. The small girl finds watercress and pulls it and smells its mineral rich goodness and begins to chew. Her eyes are full.

Absent mindedly, Girl stands and wanders back into the midst of the herd, touching here and there, scratching an ear and walking, leaning into here and her and him and the great beasts roll their eyes to watch and swish their tails to guide her along and after a time she is back with the giant who carried her through the night.

She buries her face against his furry shoulder, feeling the warmth from the sun that is held there. He smells of clean grass. She reaches to grab a handful of fur and climb, but the hide slips and there is after all, only a man who wears a robe. And it is only a robe and he and she are walking with the herd and his face is as calm as the still blue sky and his eyes are as clear and liquid as the stream.

Girl is not surprised, and she only takes the man's hand, and they continue to stroll, buffalo pace. The man begins to sing the buffalo song and the cows and bulls all around swing their heads and stamp their feet in time and occasional grunts and huffs and slapping tails against flanks are the chorus and the rhythm and the conversation.

And the girl hums and skips and all is well.

***

A teenage girl all long and lean and wild and brown and hair and lightening quick and flashing laughter and sometimes she rides and sometimes she walks and runs and dances along and through the herd. She hugs some and teases others and steers clear of a very few. These angry bulls, they cannot help themselves, some hormonal genetic innate primitive drive can come upon them at times, and they become irritable and touchy, apt to swing their head in annoyance and stamp their feet in frustration. When two who are this way come together, all give them space, making a careful circle and buffering the smaller animals from the great clashing of muscle, sinew and lust that creates violent slamming contests of mass and will and cleverness. The clashes are brief and done and things calm for a while and the herd goes about its business. The Girl does not fear these beasts at all, it is only that in those moments they can be forgetful and unrestrained, and their very size can do unintended damage to any in the wrong place. So, she is careful of them and they are careful of her and each day the man sings, and the girl now joins in and it seems a brighter song for it.

Man wears his robe more and more, longer and longer and he is loath to remove it and clearly relieved to wrap himself in it, but today he has left the hood down low on his back. It hangs heavy, forlorn, and weighs upon him and his face is somber and solemn and without joy. Man has sliced off to the side of the herd and pulled Girl with him and sitting down he weaves with his fingers and sings beneath his breath and gazes at the ground for a very long time. From deep in his robe, he retrieves a pipe, a knife, a gourd and some intricate thread of tendon and hair and grass and knots.

Man tells the girl of history. How the herd's movements have created. How to sing. How to smoke. And how to wear the robes. He gives her the threads and the knife and the gourd. He loads the pipe and tamps and shows the ground, the sky, the four directions; and Girl has made a small fire and there is a strange feeling in her chest of loss and sadness all mingled with something tender and grateful and wise.

Man looks at girl and he does not smile. He does not cry. You can see there though, the changing, the months and the years and the unexpected laughs that have erupted forth, the hard-edged terror when she was out of sight and some dreadful thing happened...a wave through the herd would say,

She is ok.

And the man would breathe again. You can see the movement of his face, all those moments somehow rippling across his visage and illuminating the goodness and the sorrow and his longing to be back in his robe. And the man lights the pipe and sings a different song and smoke rises and blows about and the man is softening, blurring and he passes the pipe to the girl who looks with great love upon the man and raises the pipe and draws deep. The orange glow brightens in the bowl and the harsh taste of smoke and the man pulling the hood over his head and there the great buffalo with his heavy head and gusting breaths and she places her cheek, for one last time on his shoulder and feels the slow ka-thump-thump beat of his massive heart and huffing exhales.

Girl exhales smoke towards the sky and it is swirling up and darkening and coalescing and becoming and there is the Raven with bright glittery eyes and glistening purple=black feathers and biting sarcasm, pointedly piercing all excuses, and speaking directly to the mind.

Raven's heart, if there is one, is small and quiet and there is only the vast absence of the great, regular, rolling rhythm of the buffalo herd heart. The whooshing and gusting, the in and out of their breath, and the low soft rumble of herd conversation are going gone now, moving away and away. And the girl is trying to reach for the man, but he is changed now for good and gone. The herd is moving, and Girl is sitting. She rests atop a fallen tree and perched near is the black raven and his critical, skeptical, eye and the girl weeps quietly for a very long time.

Raven

That night Girl is cold for the first time in years and so remembers the tools the man has given her. She builds a small fire and curls herself around its small warmth, while the raven laughs from the darkness, though not without some kindness.

Sun rises and the,

Good mornings!

Of all the birds begin and Raven is singing wake up, wake up. He is hungry, and the girl can walk, and the insects will fly to avoid her feet and he will eat.

***

Girl walks slow to the stream and washes her face in its cool forgiving waters, and she sees herself there without the man. It is a sobering sight. Girl is older and settling and becoming a new, more solid creature. She is more grave and more serene. She still laughs easily but it is a quieter, wiser laugh, softened with grief and newfound wisdom, born of heartache. These days when Raven lashes her ears with some critique, she hardly notices the tone, only takes note of the content.

Days are full and there is hunger and cold and much learning. Often Raven takes the Girl on his back and beating with his powerful wings, they fly away to other dimensions and times. The two travel sometimes high and sometimes low down to the underneath place, and hurt people live there, and lost people. Sometimes they encounter people carried on smoke or some plant and they are there in the after or the before or the high or the low, but they do not belong, they only visit with kaleidoscope eyes and awestruck hands that dance in the air pretending to play some invisible instruments.

They are the forever visitors, strangers who are not wholly anywhere. And residing elsewhere, they come only to take, to learn, to find some way through grief and heart ache, love or delusion. These visitors never stay long, and these visitors never truly arrive...ephemeral, they waft weightless on the breezes, the streams and currents that flow through the other places like strands of golden light.

These poor searching souls cannot touch, they cannot hold, only darkly see. Girl sees these wandering ghosts and pities them in her untamed way for their insubstantial nature.

Girl can hold with her hands. She can sit with the lost and gaze for hours at the veins on the backs of their hands and touch the freckles and the wrinkles and smooth the furrowed brows. Girl brings food and warmth and while the denizens of these other places do not run to greet her, they are always happy when she comes to visit.

And Raven sits brittle and black. Perched on his branch of remove, he allows these experiences, these hours, and he watches and waits.

Death

Morning comes, and Girl watches the sun announce itself and then rise, brilliant purple, pink and orange fire greeting the planet with life. She sighs and looks at her own hands and feet and some melancholy song erupts from her throat and she sings a story so full of question and longing that morning birds go quiet and still, then gather close to listen. And the raven flies straight through her sounds and flapping unrepentant wings, he shatters the air and fractures it and scoops the girl up and travels through the thin curtain and they are sitting on a branch, in a tree, a birch tree...white and silver bark with dark splashes and barren twigs and below in the snow stands a buffalo on quivering legs.

The ground is churned and turned and thrashed from his desperate spinning and flailing hooves. There are splashes of dark red, thick, and steaming and each heavy rasping exhale sprays new droplets of red in every direction. This bull is an old one and sick, and the wolves are closing in. The bull has stopped turning to face the pack and only stands, chest heaving like a bellows, blowing vast huffing breathes in and out, and his head hangs low from the weight and the worry and time.

This buffalo's eyes roll frantically this way and that and the girl leaps from her branch to go to him, but Raven holds her back and will not let her go. She turns to him angry and demands release, but Raven only points his hard, shiny beak towards the terrible scene below and sits. The wolves, cautious, close in from all sides, the great wounded animal will soon be down. Still, a wayward hooking horn or powerful slashing hoof and it will be the end for some unfortunate wolf.

Girl is filled with sorrow and outrage.

How unfair!!!

And she struggles to free herself and rush to Buffalo's aid.

Buffalo sees Girl there high on a branch and bellows forth the song of his people. It begins strong enough but quickly devolves into a coughing sputter, then fades into a sad, hurt, moan. Girl, on her branch, thrashes about wildly enough that the wolves stare up at her. Their eyes slow her racing heart and still her thrashing about and they let out a very few notes of their own song.

Girl, eyes wide, looks to the bull and in sorrow and mourning, begins to sing the Buffalo song. Her heart is swelling with the size of the feeling, and soon, so full she cannot hold back her tears, her song sounds a grief-stricken cry, a hurt filled eulogy. The sad last story of the Buffalo nation.

From time long before and now and time stretching forward as far as the plains, there has always been change. We each and all, participate in that change and the herd goes on as far as the eye can reach. She sings a comfort song and a belonging song and there the old, the middle and the new walk one alongside the another.

The great old bull looks to the wolves. His eyes are no longer wild with fear. And the wolves, they can see their hungry cubs hidden amongst the low firs. They feel the raw irritation of those tiny confused and empty stomachs and so they summon all their courage. With a determined cry the pack launches themselves forward. Pulling on the bull's tail, trying to find his thin, vulnerable, legs, swarming on and over and under the old bull until there is only one giant beast of grey and black, white and red and snarling and protesting and in the middle of the end the old bull's eye connects on a line, on a thread, straight to the Girl and her heart is beating as fast as his and bitter tears are streaming down her face and her heart pounds against her ribs seeking only to escape her very chest and fly down to be with this dying bull. But Girl can only sing loud and louder, and the mourning and the passing is terrifying and then over.

The wolves are exhausted and bruised yet they sit and raise their muzzles high to sing the bull to the next place, to his new home, and to thank him for feeding their children. And the cubs peek out of the bush and carefully move into the open and the adults are tearing open the tough old flesh and the cubs are yipping and hungry and the alpha says *okay*, and they close in and eat. And the mother wolves they look up at the girl. She is quiet now and though tears still fall she does not sob, and she does not thrash to be free.

The bull's death brings life and the old nourishes the new and the river of time flows ever onward and the knowing of this, the learning of this brings a quiet and painful understanding. Even Raven is silent.

In this way.

In these ways the Raven transports the Girl and shows her and teaches.

Death.

Girl lives a waking dream. So often they penetrate the thin veil that lies between now and another now, upper, middle, lower, and so easily she moves between and in the seeing she is fearless and moves as a ghost. A touch for comfort there, a passing brushing of the hair out of someone's eyes, these rituals of connection and care become her habit and no animal fears her. Even trees and grasses bend towards her.

And in all these times she walks where she will.

And Raven is satisfied.

Tree

Is it strange that a tree should become Girl's teacher? And is it strange that Girl has become Young Woman?

She is not the tallest, nor the roundest and she is definitely not the oldest tree amongst the grove, perhaps this is why she deigned speak to the Young Woman. The older, taller fatter giants with their crowns so high they smell the ocean and see the edge, are almost too gone to speak human terms. They are in between the eternal and the never was and having stood for so long have largely lapsed into silence, a deep appreciative, mindless state of being only witnessing all, more awed by God's creation than those whose observations have not been as lengthy. The giants are removed from the ordinary, permanently bridged all the way into the heavens. But Young Tree spoke. And the now Young Woman is moved to tears and she does sit, down upon soft needles, shaded by wide branch and cradled by enormous roots.

Young Woman rests, and Raven cocks his head and he does not smile but he swells himself with self-satisfaction and fluffs his feathers and strides back and forth until Woman reaches her hand out to caress his shiny blue-black feathers and he does scoff, though not with his usual enthusiasm and flies away.

Tree whispers, and Tree sighs and underneath there is a deep resonant groaning. Low vibrations that play the body like a drum and a humming frequency too low to hear, rearranging cells and molecules and small tendrils, tiny sprouts erupting forth and Medicine Girl does swoon and lean hard against Tree.

The touch of the deep red rust colored skin, the spongy feeling and the loamy smell and the soft depth of the forest floor and then sinking onto her back, and the light waving in beams through the grand branches, limbs, and feeling sensory organs, all precede a deep groaning and creaking sound. And suddenly the earth is raw and new and there are the strangest of creatures near. There comes the smell of some burning and sulphureous, yellow air, and the cracking of the crust and spraying forth of the red molten rock and the cold time and great hairy beasts and people with strange thick faces.

Where does knowledge come from? There is a rising and falling of life and system and the Young Woman sees into the persons and the cells and closer, deeper, farther into the spiraling ladder and memories there and she recognizes the patterns, the symbols the shapes and unconsciously traces them in the air with her fingers lighter than a down feathers touch. Tree moans in some ecstatic taste, first blush of awakening, and her roots travel farther, and her limbs reach higher and there are audible creaks and pops and cracking as they grow.

Young Woman travels down into the remains of older plants changed, down into the dirt and the fungi there and is swept along like flotsam on a creek, a stream, a river, an ocean of flashing light into the vast center of an incomprehensibly large information exchange. The stories are as simple as,

I am hurt.

Here is food.

We are with you, we are with you; you are not alone.

And these simple stories are as rich and nuanced, as full of love and texture as any story, anywhere. They are as complete. And the Young Woman feels tears trace the curves of her cheek and she feels...all. A symphonic peace that is at once her and beginning inside her and at the same time all. Every miracle has its place and its part and there is no space only fabric and she is reminded and remembering over and over, again and again, beyond connection to oneness and a movement here ripples throughout everywhere and so in real time, there is no time, only a vantage point from which one sees or does not.

Sighing into wakefulness, the small girl, the tiny girl who holds all these secrets, hitches and sobs with a gratitude and joy larger than she can hold. And it is delirious and inarticulate and so true that the tall trees welcome her, and she can see with their eyes the vast forest, the foggy cliffs where ocean splashes blue green and white froth, shattering itself over and over with rapturous abandon. She is lifted up, and the breeze which has no start, and no end dries her face of tears and bathes her in energies from heaven and earth and the tall trees are singing the same songs as the Young Woman and it is enough to reside here.

Rooted in oneness, lifting straight into a gratitude so profound it is god like. And Eagle swoops by and brushes her neck, a gentle touch of his wing. And Young Woman rides on his back, down to the ground and stands there facing Tree.

The lessons of Tree. Young Woman learns.

Sunshine is life. Water is life. Live high amongst the angels but have roots which connect you to the ground and the tribe. Shelter those who need it.

Soft, soft upon the earth to go quietly, moving not with subterfuge but with awe...seeing hearing smelling tasting feeling the barrier of flesh as no barrier so that the energies flow, ebb and swell. Swelling heart and moving out from the center. Animals fall and approach and come for a scratch or to offer a treat or just to be near and the Young Woman stands like the tree hour after hour, day after day, feeling the fog turn to dew, turn to drops of water, shiny, round magnifying droplets resting cool on feverish skin and tangled hair.

Breezes soft, kiss, caress, wash through her and away. First her skin becomes soft and her features smooth. Soon her neck, spine and knees straighten. Her feet submerge in fallen pine and tiny flowers burst up through the forest floor like tiny blue and white stars. Young Woman attends the church of the wood. She stands until her bones align and muscles release. Her every pulsing heartbeat driving, swaying, rounding, rolling, infinity signs of deeper and deeper relaxation. Each breath a shift in her center of gravity. Her center of gravity becoming ever more and more right here, right inside, and the forest revolves around her, and the continent and the planet and the universe and there standing holding some center, She is all of it, alive as an expression of self-awareness, bearing witness to itself. Small blue dragonfly lands on her fingertips. Sparrow rests upon her shoulder. And squirrel lays across her foot, content to be close to Creatress, creation.

Young Woman soars in the space between galaxies.

Timelessness.

Choosing a thin thread, she turns and follows and swirling down and down remembers herself standing in the meadow that turns golden in the midst of storm. In the night and low, she hears Tree singing ecstatic hymns. Longing, Young Woman feels a longing, a yearning want and cannot describe why or from whence this small, empty space comes. And shaking herself she shudders and looks at the blue night around. And the frogs sing, and the crickets play. It seems that even the clouds make some roughing noise as they slide across the sky. Young Woman moves, and Coyote calls the very sound, the very feeling that she holds deep in her belly and so she goes to him there, to see.

***

Coyote does not mourn, he is instead a happy trickster, yet each night he searches for Moon in the Sky and takes his moments to sit, point his nose to the light and yodel out this longing, this feeling of distinction. And Young Woman understands that it is this separation, this momentary delusion of being only a piece of it and not the all of it, the large of it, that generates a convulsing of her diaphragm and a constricting of her ribcage and a sound being drawn out of her very soul, the spark, the place where all is still ALL.

Young Woman yodels her own separateness into the night sky. And she feels the beginnings of a heat, a desire to possess another, to hold another, so close beyond close, in a merging act, that, if only for moments, flashes like the big bang and dissolves any illusion of distinction.

The animals say a storm is coming. They stay low to the ground, tidy their nests, and make last minute checks on food supplies. Young Woman can feel it coming, too, a pregnant waiting, a stillness that can almost make the ears pop, a small stirring of the leaves, of the grasses and a quickening of the pulse, a rising of the hairs on the arm and the back of the neck and a sipping sound with each inhale.

A storm is coming, and Young Woman feels electrified and energized and pulled towards the low-pressure place. And tossing her hair, she rolls her things and stuffs them under the great big rock, a hiding place, a safe place. Her cheeks are flushing, and her lips, they thicken. Urgency comes to her and she thrills and laughs and runs on the very tops of trees and dances across the empty spaces. A storm IS coming, and Young Woman is eager.

Bad Man

Abandoned

Snow, falling heavy and wet, clings to the branches
of the weary green trees, pulling, weighing down
and falling from the branches, drifting, and piling up
in banks of icy quiet. The woman staggers through
the deep snow holding her little bundle, her little
man close to her chest, clutching him tightly as a
secret, holding him near enough to share foggy
breath. Stumbling, she looks about. It is as far as
she can go. Any farther and she will lay down and
give up and die and she must not.

There, a spot under the low hemlock green and white that is almost a cave. Drifts circle the trunk and stack and rise, eddy and swirl and there is the place. She crawls awkwardly over and collapses under the shelter of giant branches and squeezes the tiny bundle, holds the tiny boy close one last time. She does not cry.

The woman understands that this is no fairy tale, no psychological circumstance. The boy must go. And he will most certainly die. She hopes he doesn't suffer much, but hope is a fleeting and furtive emotion for her; hope brings pain, hope brings swift punishment and so is best kept hidden and silent, buried under deep drifts of snow so that even its cries are muffled, smothered and choked until every hope lies as cold and still as death.

She places the small package, the small boy, in the shelter of the space underneath the heavy, snow laden branches. He is surrounded by piled high drifts and lays on the few inches of snow that even here covers the ground. The woman does not look at the boy's face. As she turns to go, he reaches out his small hand and grasps at her shawl. She hesitates for a moment, ducks her head, exhales what may have been a sob and crawls back out from under the tree and stands. She gives the large branch a hard tug and snow falls with a heavy thump. She does not look back, only walks away in the direction of her own empty fate.

The small boy is wide open. Is it disbelief? Confusion? He does not know...fear yes...but, maybe, just maybe, a bit of awe. Some spark of understanding hardens his eyes, even at his tender age he instinctively respects the callousness, the unrepentant, unrelenting mastery of all feeling in service to one's own life. It is simple. His father was killed, butchered, and tortured while he and his mother were forced to watch. The man who killed his father took his mother and she had one choice. Become his or die. A terrible simplicity. Clean as a cut. She was told to pack her things and kill the boy. She brushed aside thought and packaged him and walked out into the bitter true, cold white winter, both as relentless, as remorseless as death.

Now the small boy child lies, curled and close, shivering underneath his blanket of snow. And his eyes are the strangest sight, they are dark and grey as a stormy sky and somehow still. The small boy wallows around and with his own will and rage creates a small cave. He will consider. He will live.

All through the night the young boy sits, rocking to stay warm. Through all the dark hours he sits in the absolute darkness, surrounded by frozen water, encased in this frozen tomb, this icy womb; and he feels the pull and the warm call to surrender and wills it away. And the cold, he accepts the cold, breathes it in, allows it to touch his skin where it has snuck through folds and thin spots and he sits unblinking and draws the cold in deeper. He decides that he will not hurt if he becomes as cold as the snow.

When day light makes his snow cave brighter, he pushes forward and fights his way out and into the open.

Bad Man Born

The small boy crawls out into the bright, frigid day. He sits quietly for a moment and then stands and begins to move down, down slope. The white snow glare burns his eyes, and the sun warms his clothing and his skin. He winces as the edges of his toes begin to thaw but moves on.

The small, lonely boy has learned a sort of alchemy. He transforms pain and discomfort into an anger, an all-consuming, simmering rage. He cultivates hate as his motivating force, and it is powerful enough to make hunger and thirst, even cold, irrelevant. He only eats, drinks, and builds fire to survive, to move forward.

Forward and down, stumbling through drifts as high as his tiny chest, one step then another and then, some hours later the small boy finds the low line of a partially frozen water way. There are still fresh tracks in the snow, in the black, stiff mud. Searching about the small boy locates and lifts and slams a rock down hard, smashing the icy, frozen edge of the stream, creating a cracking, splashing sound and then cries out as if in pain. He finds a thin slice of stone, a shard, and slices a thin cut down the outside of his arm, lays down on his back and forces sobbing noises through his tight throat.

Holding tightly to the stone and the shard and waiting... he allows himself to feel the exhaustion of the night, of the cold. He searches and finds the hollow place where surrender used to live and moving there, he uses the memory, and mimics and moans the sounds of despair and pain. Soon enough, the predators appear. They are cautious, humans are the most dangerous animal in this forest and this small pack has learned to be leery. The second wolf smells the copper blood smell, and the frail human is only moaning now, barely even breathing. Emboldened, he approaches too quickly, too certain, and as he nears the boy, head low and sniffling, he lifts his head, turns to look at his pack members, to invite and the small boy smashes the rock into the side of the wolf's head stunning him for a moment, a long enough moment. The boy uses the same rock to smash the wolf's foot and as the wolf howls in pain, he grasps its fleeing tail and smashes another foot and wolf is down, snarling and yelping in some dawning expression of fear, rage and pain.

The pack had begun their closing in, but they freeze at this abrupt turn of fortune. The boy, instead of moaning and crying is charging, and the pack is retreating, and the injured wolf is scrabbling and scratching and trying to move, but he cannot on his mangled and broken feet.

The boy feels his blood pulsing thick and fast through his veins. Primal hunger makes his mouth water. He watches as the wolf thrashes about trying to find some way to flee, to attack, anything to end this terrible suffering. The boy only finds a large boulder, climbs up and sits to think.

Later he will collect the wood and build the fire and butcher the wolf, but for the moment he just sits and watches with deep curiosity the wolf's struggle and pain. Cruelty crawls through him like a snake, coiling and slithering and filling him with some strange hissing pleasure. The boy is becoming.

***

Springtime dirt smells different, richer, thick with a strange mixture of death churning and roiling over into the genesis of life, the makings of new growth created by mother earth's alchemy. This a wisdom older than any memory. A cosmic religion of immutable law that is a circle, a wheel, a turning and rolling over and over, a plow tilling and turning deep.

And the boy sits still on his familiar, small boulder, listening to the growing stream. It rushes gleefully over the small rocks and swirls around the newest trees, falling down the mountain, down the hill, released from the winter snowpack, free, free to tumble trickle roar splash and leap into the air with frothy white happiness, all the way to the great water. And he thinks.

People

Winter has passed, He has survived. Winter has passed and yesterday the boy saw footprints and followed and there was a young girl walking along the bank searching for blackberries or blue berries or anything really. Her fanciful, worry free footwork and her obvious flights of fascination with every little sign of life and color, kept her in a state of wonder so all-encompassing that she did not notice the still boy watching her from the shadows of the forest's edge. And now the boy recognizes his dilemma. She represents human beings, a clan or herd or tribe of people. On the one hand the most fearsome predators in this land, on this land, an untrustworthy lot, full of inexplicable passions and violence and yet, at the same time; an alliance with people will provide the boy his best chance for survival and long-term security.

Green, green leaves, green grass, all explosions of color and life rising up, breaking out, breaking free from the cold. The white snow is shrinking from the warm light of the sun, retreating to hide in the shady spots beneath trees and under rocks and losing and leaving, resentfully, disappearing until next winter.

The boy has survived. He is thin, exhausted, and frail in appearance. But he has survived to sit here and bask in the sun like a snake absorbing heat, absorbing energy into his skin, his muscles, and bones, perhaps even into his very heart and soul.

The small boy shudders and feels some great coldness, some vast emptiness leaving. He is filling up with warmth and hope, rounding and fattening like the animal's bellies who gorge on the new shoots and berries and feast on the weak, and new creatures who cannot yet run or fight. And so, he sits here on his overlook, watching the stream splash by, its crashing waters practically shouting delight.

***

The boy has watched as the village warriors make their way across the stream, leaving the camp and yet close enough still that they are not overly cautious. He sees the snorting, head shaking horses blowing steam and dancing with nervous pent-up energy, ready for the hunt. Winter, the long cold sleep has passed.

Soon thereafter, trailing in those warriors' wake, the small boys come, skipping and stalking and leaping from stone to stone, shoving and wrestling and growing into themselves and full and shoving their chests out with pride and masking any fears they may feel with whoops and jokes and bravado. These small warriors are followed closely by mothers picking their way down to the stream and washing and scolding and hiding their smiles. Last to arrive are the young girls laughing and watching everything, every, thing, missing nothing and it is one of them who first spots the tiny, frail, disheveled boy and cries out and points.

The boy is caught off guard and, in his surprise, he sprints away into the high tree forest where has lived for these last months. He is gone before anyone on the stream can really register anything about him.

There is a stir and a fuss and much conversation about what to do about the strange child living alone in the woods and no one has a good answer or even any idea how to proceed. The warriors have done their reconnaissance before leaving for the hunting and found no nearby villages or roaming parties, so the consensus is that the boy must be alone, but how could he have survived the cold of winter? How indeed. The security pickets are informed and alerted to keep an extra eye out for any threat and maybe for the small boy himself. The young girls are full of stories and rumors of the boy's origins and the mothers are tut-tutting about the poor child who will surely die if left alone.

The young village boys are convinced the young boy is an enemy, one to be hunted down and killed. And so, they form a war party and set out from the village in the early morning to hunt and end the boy.

He watches them painting themselves and ramping themselves up emotionally and then heading out into the forest as a group, hopelessly naïve, so noisy that no healthy animal will ever not flee before them.

As they pass harmlessly by, the boy ponders. He is perched in a tall tree, high above the boys watching their carefully constructed courage and peer inflated bravado.

He could lead these boys. They could hunt down the man who murdered his father and exact slow, happy revenge. The boy shakes his head, he has no trust for humans. And though he longs for the comfort of the familial lodge filled with the smells of cooking food and fire and human beings he knows he cannot reach across that divide and trust ever again.

She

She moves by as a center, as the eye of some powerful storm. Dense cloud bands spin out and off and away from her and touch everything. The boy's heart stops, and he cannot breathe. And he feels a flutter as when falling from the high cliff and into the icy cold waters. He feels the shock and numbness as though splashing softly into a place of clarity and beauty and an all-encompassing, no place left untouched, immersion in Her. The boy staggering, stumbles, out of the forest and into plain view. Pulled along by the gravitational field that is her, he staggers into the village center. And so complete is his fascination with the girl that no one is even alerted to his presence, no one is alarmed. He, enveloped by her, is invisible and he floats on numb, unseeing feet until there is a gasp.

The girl turns and smiles, and the boy falls to his knees and sits and the mothers rush to wrap up the girl and surround her in their protective bunch. The picket sentries rush to the calling and slide to a stop, standing unsure, unclear as to procedure here. There is a tiny boy on his knees here, hard to distinguish from the dirt here, a new thing.

The boy's frail brown frame is living breathing desperation and in his eyes are pictures of a bleak, mad, future. He shudders violently with the pain of hope, and cries. Tears roll down the boy's cheeks, rivulets tracking through his dusty face. And he knows not why, cannot say why, and no words will come. His heart is a butterfly, a hummingbird flipping and buzzing from flower to flower, and She fills his eyes, and he can barely breathe.

Strong hands grasp the boy's arms and pull him roughly to his feet. He shakes himself and the two warriors yelp and bounce back hopping up and down on one foot. A hand is raised and falling strikes the tiny bird boy and he is down on his face, on his back and fighting to regain his feet when the old man says,

Stop.

And the tiny bird boy sees the girl's eyes widen with fright, and so he stills and stands with dark eyes and red lightening on his cheek. The two men, chagrined and rueful, rub shins that were kicked hard and arms that were scratched deep. And the old man shuffles forward to the tiny frail boy and looks upon him.

The boy, tiny or no, is a force, a natural thing like an avalanche or a thunderstorm, a cloud floating overhead or a thorny flower. The Old Man knows.

Old Man

In the new spring heat, with all the rushing and vibration and feeling and fear, with all of his despair and the weight of his hope, the tiny boy struggles to stay on his feet, but stay on his feet he does. The Old Man approaches him and searching the boy's face, offers water and food, but the boy does not move.

Old Man is covered in tattoos and lines that shift and move and somehow mimic the stars above. He smells of resins and herbs and sweet grasses and he alone of all the people stands as still as the boy. They watch one another, and by some unspoken agreement when the old man turns, the young boy follows. Old Man walks slowly back to his lodge and stoops and enters the smoky, fragrant space, never once looking back. The boy will follow or not. Fate and the great wheel have brought the boy here, moments such as these are far beyond any beckoning.

Inside, the old man motions for Boy to sit, but Boy does not. He only stands staring at the old man through quick, liquid brown eyes. Without any hurry, without any sign, Old Man drops the hide that serves as a door. The shelter's interior is dark but for the light spotting down from the very center of the lodge. Grey smoke swirls and tiny motes of dust float and waft and eddy and come together and coalesce. Now the motes have become a cloud, a thick cloud, turning and swooping round the lodge, denser and closer until Raven is caroming around and flaring to a stop to perch atop the old man's crown. Turning his head sideways Raven glares at the boy for long moments and then pressing down with its feet he launches towards the boy and *flap* hits him in the forehead, in the face, in the eyes, with one wing and the boy is knocked backwards, falling.

After one breath, after a thousand stampeding heart beats, the boy loses the sensation of falling, rather he is drifting through some starless sky, black and cold and quiet. Spiraling color holes spin in front his eyes. He is traveling.

Horror

The boy is crouched low, hugging the earth, trying hard to become the dirt. He has no thought only a fervent desire to disappear, disappear here under this bush. And there is a shrinking and a crackling, shifting moment and Boy has become the weasel. He twitches his long, furry tail and each inhale delivers information, it floats on every current and layer of the wind. This nightmare day's vibrations tickle his whiskers, and the boy/ weasel shakes his head. There, his father is crawling, clawing, and scratching his way forward towards his wife, beseeching. The boy sees the dirt wet with his father's blood become mud. He sees his father's cracked fingernails find purchase and pull.

A strange man strides forward and straddling the fallen man, looks down on the boy's father's back, the broad warm back that Boy has ridden mile upon mile after sunny laughing mile. The stranger grasps a handful of dark hair and pulls father's head back stretching the neck and exposing the throat to the point of breaking. The strange man stabs down into the shoulder joint and father cries out. Mother buries her face in her hands and wails, a hard, broken keening that rises like the chill of terror up the small boy's spine.

The strange man pulls the point of the knife down, etching a thin red line, opening a red and pink slash that fills with dark blood. The awful man continues, trailing the point of his knife over to the spine, probing each vertebra and finding there, the one he seeks, presses slowly down, into and separating, shearing. The nerves are broken, and father's legs go limp.

There is a follow-on surrendering sort of resignation that flows over and through his father's impractical body. And father drops his face into the dirt and closes his hand and grasps the dust and the grass and feels eternity there. Mother is collapsed on the ground and done, no longer present, vacant, haunted, sha has become a ghost. And she, the ghost, is looking up at the stranger who is carving around bones and gone and adrift she nods,

Yes! Yes. Okay, only stop...

And the stranger, with unchanging face, plunges the knife once more into father's spine, high and around and stabbing, piercing into the artery and his father's life is pulse pumping out into the dirt. And small, the boy darts around the bottom of the bush, a weasel, a long lithe dark furry hissing thing, and he would attack but who? And a feral, harsh, high anger screams out of him and the strange man throws his knife hard. And the weasel/ boy sees nothing after, only darkness.

**

Once again, the small, frail, force of nature is standing in the Old Man's lodge and shaking, not trembling but shuddering, vibrating. The tiny earthquake boy is rattling the bones and the pipes and all the things the Old Man has collected, and the people are stunned and frightened, reaching to hold their children close. Only the Old Man sits calmly, unmoved, unafraid, solemn. He bears witness.

The tiny mad boy wizard calms and stands still in front of the Old Man and he is unaware of the tears carving shiny, sparkly paths down his darkened face and falling from his chin.

The Old Man motions for the child to sit and so he does.

Gifts

Old Man holds close his tools and flavors, feathers, and bones. He tamps the tobacco tight in the bowl and summons the spark and then the small flame. Thin blue smoke begins to swirl and dance about, lifting, and floating motes of dust up and higher to make a kaleidoscope sky of tiny stars.

And, in a moment, the black and blue lines that decorate Old Man's body begin to move and bend, twirl and swirl and rising up and away from the skin the lines curl and carve and describe shapes, Universal shapes. The black and blue lines that were on the Old Man's skin shift color and change to orange and yellow and blue light. The Old Man sits quietly and the lines, the floating shapes circle round the boy closer and closer until they alight on his skin and he is marked. There is a burning smell, and he is floating rising thinning and swirling out of the top of the lodge. He is looking down and seeing the people there below. They are still somewhat shaken by the boy's small quakes. Boy sees the girl there below and feels his heart leap out like a free bird leaping from a high cliff to fly. Swooping over it all, he keeps rising and seeing. Boy sees and does know the vast valley and the mountains and the plains spreading far, the herds and masses of buffalo and caribou and flocks of geese and birds swirling through the sky and demonstrating the very same shapes and design and fluid flowing symbols as the ones newly now, covering his body.

Then there, amidst his flight, he spies two single humans. He touches first the small girl child frightened and all alone in the high forest, uncertain, afraid. Boy experiences her pulsing sadness and her fundamental fear and insecurity. He tastes her hopes and wishes, dreams and delusions and Boy is feeling her feelings and filling with her power and growing larger and larger, large as a cloud.

And there an old man sitting sheltered by the pine branch and singing in the, I have passed through weakness and returned to strength, voice of the death songs; the come and take me to next songs. The boy sinks down and low and surrounds the old one and is absorbed by, fascinated by the strength and the allowing and the giving over to the next.

This is all very confusing to the Boy and he is shrinking and being swept by the winds back and back until he is pulled down into the Old Man's lodge. There, sitting and gasping for breath, he watches the Old Man's eyes open, and he sees himself through the Old Man's eyes and he closes his own and rests.

In these moments, the boy comes to know who he is.

***

There are other moments, moments where the boy completely forgets himself and falling, follows the girl, fascinated by her every move. She ties bright colored ribbons in all the horse's manes; and he, mesmerized, hangs on every single, mindfully tied knot. Boy watches so closely that he times his own inhales and exhales with the rising and falling of the girl's ribs. Boy is medicine born and so allowed the freedom to watch, to see, to be anywhere. The hunt holds no special interest for him, though the kill itself was interesting once. Boy was there as the life left the animal. He saw it, touched it, tasted it, and felt the invigoration as a sustenance.

The girl tries to honor tradition. She understands the privilege granted medicine folk. When Boy stares at her with his barely banked fire stare, she only looks at the ground with wide eyes and wonder before returning to whatever task involves her. But on occasion she becomes frightened and flutters and flaps and shrinks away from the boy with involuntary revulsion. In those moments, the small boy darkens, his eyes flash and clouds in the sky move irregularly. Animals become skittish and shake and hop frantic and frenzied all around. When and then, Boy will close his eyes and sip air deep, the tremors will stop, and the clouds recede. He is only a small child after all, lonely and full of wonder.

In those moments, the girl sees all of him. She sees that he is fragile, as breakable as the finest shell, transparent and opaque to the light. Part of her, some, in her belly instinct, wants to protect him and hold him safe and chase away the ones who stare and gawk from the edges of their vision. Boy feels her shift and weeps. Boy tender and touched, emits some glowing, lovely thing that makes anyone near want to gather around and bathe in this love, this pure vulnerability. And the dogs do. When the small boy cries, the village dogs lean against him, press their foreheads against his legs and lay at his feet and on his feet.

And when Boy falls asleep the dogs gather close around him and it is impossible to say who is warming whom. The people might do the same except that they fear his awakening and his all-seeing eyes.

In time, Old Man's lessons give way to remembering and traveling. No longer do the two wizards sit talking in the Old Man's lodge. Moving out into the forest green and brown and soft with life and death and clean and eternally circling with waste, renewal and birth, a state of melancholy moves in and soon they barely speak, only travel together. Soaring over ice caps and strange white bears, across vast bodies of water and seeing the strange people that live there and to their favorite spots, the pair fly to their favorite energies and there they just sit. Old Man napping, young Boy never impatient, only sighing and dreaming of the village girl as the days while away.

Old Man Dies

There is a special quiet that comes just before dawn. Mist floats in the low areas, covering creeks and valley. Dew glistens on every surface, trembling and sparking like a billion tiny diamonds. There are no more flames in the fire pit, only the dark edged glow of embers not yet ready to wake and go to work.

It is during this pre-dawn in between that the young boy stirs, and startles awake. He feels the fire on his skin, as a burning. He smells his burning flesh and fiery hair, and it is an awful smell. But as bad as the smell is, it is not the largest sensation. Boy is overwhelmed by the searing pain of the ancient lines being drawn, etched, burned into his skin. He screams aloud in agony and writhes in his blanket and the dogs flee, tails between their legs and whimpers in their throats. There is a great shaking of the earth. The people run from their lodges, eyes wide and full, searching the heavens, clinging to one another like flotsam in a storm-tossed sea. The shaking deepens and the people cower and collect in groups and the men grip their weapons tightly as if to ward off some deliberately dangerous beast, but there is no wild thing here, only the insane howling of the young boy becoming a Young Man Wizard as the symbols burn onto and cut into him. The vast opening is to him, pain. He is only one long and ceaseless howl.

Young Man Wizard

At last, the Young Man can stand, and he stagger stumbles towards the Old Man's lodge and the people watch him on his way. Some cannot stifle their cries nor still their tremors, but the Young Man Wizard does not notice, so consumed with his new eyes, that he cannot really access his old ones. Stumbling as a blind man, Young Man fumbles his way to the Old Man's lodge and falls against the flap, inhaling, exhaling, sweeping aside the blanket there and stopping.

Inside the lodge all is still, even smoke does not move but hangs suspended in time. The Old Man's blankets are empty and there is only a small package of herbs and bones and secrets collected from a lifetime of magic, resting where the Old Man has placed it for the Young Man to inherit. He is gone.

***

It cannot be said that the Young Man ever loved the Old, but he had certainly sheltered under Old Man's lofty branches, free of the knowledge and the sight that the tallest of trees must bear. Now that protection is gone, and the Young Man, blinded in a sense, unable to see as he had before, is seeing the essential things. He sees the glowing, and watches as the different colors stream forth from life and swirl round objects. Young Man collapses onto the ground and covers his eyes with his palms and scrubs and shouts aloud, cursing death and sight and alone. Alone.

For four days the Young Man does not leave Old Man's lodge. When he can at last move, he sits up and then, rocking in place he sings. Songs the Old Man had taught him of the next and the leaving. He sings the songs of becoming too. For whatever he had been before? He now no longer is. In the dark of the lodge, Young Man watches as all things animate or no, emit their light, their sounds and the waves of movement that connect all things.

Young Man sees how even in the remotest of places the lights are displaced as he inhales, how the swirl of his exhales play all the way out to the edges of his vision and beyond. He is here and aware as his perspective expands. Young Man sees how hours and moments go by like water in a stream and to him it seems that if you are a strong enough swimmer, you might even swim upstream.

The veil between realms seems thinner than ever and Young Man visits dark places and sees his father there. He watches and is filled with sadness and weeps. He bears witness as his mother walks through the deep snow searching, always searching, and the Young Man carries his feeling of despising weakness like a rock on his back. The feeling rubs his flesh, leaves scars, and Young Man vows that he will never allow himself to be helpless again.

Journey after journey the hours go by and then Young Man is returning to the lodge. The Old Man's ghost is speaking and singing. Somehow Old Man's voice is no longer quavering but strong and deep and reverberating through the Young Man's being and still teaching, still comforting and Young Man goes, and Old Man is there and sitting at council and smoking the pipe. The Old Man stares long into the glow of the stones until his face is cracking from the heat and he too is something like a stone.

On the fourth day the Young Man lay in the lodge and breathed.

***

The Young Man, who sweeps aside the lodge opening and steps out into the sunlight, is a very different being than the young man who had entered only four days ago. That *before* Young Man had been shattered by pain and grief and loss. That young man had been stunned into a stupor, unsure how to navigate this now with all its strange dancing, swimming, streaming lights. He knows now that what he witnesses is a continuous connecting flow. This Young Man is pale and thin and has the lines, the shapes burned or etched deeply into his skin, and beyond his skin, into his way of perceiving. This new Young Man sees that there are no simple objects, meant only to be used, but that every substance, every being is connected. The new Man Wizard sees that when one plucks here, the ALL vibrates everywhere. He knows that a deep understanding of one thing, makes it possible to change all things.

And so, the people could see, that though he could barely stand, this Man was the Medicine Man, the one who could heal or haunt, bless or condemn. And they came and offered their tobacco and their gifts. They kept their eyes pointed downward and spoke in whispers, hoping that the Medicine Man would not make the earth shake or turn them into a lizard. And Man accepted this place and he saw who was afraid and who was calculating and who was mostly annoyed, ready to get on with the hunt. And the Medicine Man did not flinch from the things that he saw, for he understands now that he can play reality as musicians play flutes. Medicine Man knows that he can create any song he desires. And when the girl/ young woman comes with her offering, he knows that he wants her. And so, he plucks the right strings and strikes the correct rhythms, and the girl is become bewitched.

In this way the Medicine Man becomes close with the young woman and their lives begin to entwine.

For all his power and sight, Medicine Man is still shaken at his center, racked with insecurity and certain that nothing loved will last. He lays his weight on the young woman and clings to her. The young woman becomes his roots, his tree. And Medicine Man, like a vine, wraps himself around her and climbs to heights here to for unknown to him. He cannot yet see that the vine chokes the tree.

Dawn does not break; instead, the sun softly rises, as if it too is slow to be done with sleep.

Still, eventually warming and rousing to the job, sun climbs slowly up, into the morning sky.

And the coyotes yip, yip, songs are a chorus, a choir, and the light ...there is the hawk swoop swirling through the sky with deep brown wings and luminous rust colored tail...and these, these are ecstatic experiences.

No painter save God could color the grasses so that it is impossible to tell if they are white or silver, golden or brown and still have starkly dark branches and fluttery silver leaves. There are ornate religions, with brightly colored baubles and fancy smoke made to mimic the cloud and stone. There are sweet grasses to be burned to cover the smell of the crowd and displace the memory of clean air and bright flower. They are only and ever pale, weak reflections of the real thing.

But for Medicine Man there are canyon cathedrals and forest glen chapels and the blue, blue sky as wide, wider than the entire world. There is worship, each breath an expression of gratitude, each step on the earth a prayer full of hope.

***

Dawn is his time of practice. The ancients have said that the twilight regions surrounding sun rise and sun fall are filled with power. Medicine Man is certain that they are correct.

Medicine Man does understand that to begin is to go outward, into the nature. Unprotected is the only way. He must be vulnerable to the energies offered by the waking birds, the warming soil and subtle breeze. And so, he watches as the last stars become invisible, their light drowned out for the moment by a larger, closer sun. He knows they are still there, the stars. After all these years he has faith that they are not gone forever only momentarily obscured. Yes, it is true, Medicine Man has traveled far and lost sight of precious things, but he believes that the lost are still there, temporarily hidden from view, but shining none the less.

To stand like a tree, he sends roots deep into earth. Earth is the nurturer, terrestrial mother to us all, and by rooting there, Medicine Man may understand that compassion is a foundational tenant, and strong. A place to grow from. Medicine Man lifts his crown, stretching towards the heavens, lengthening his spine, lifting towards the sky, being pulled up into that heavenly space. His mind expands into the solar system's vast distances, then the galaxy, then galaxies. The universe is indescribably immense and not silent despite what some say. Medicine Man listens to emptiness sing its songs. Like a great lonely whale, it waits for him to sing back.

And Medicine Man raises his arms like branches, lower than the heavens, still high above the dirt. He is balanced between heaven and earth and his arms shelter those beneath.

Deeper in practice, Medicine Man begins to slowly move, his breath says when. He knows that the lines carved into his skin are a codex; that, hidden within those curves are the movements, are the shapes of all power. With his legs powerfully rooted and grounded, he becomes practical. With his crown lifted, he is light and loose, elusive and fluid. For the Medicine Man, obstacles no longer block or obscure, only offer new paths to explore.

***

You're quite beautiful when you move that way.

Turning to see, the woman is there. She stands just so.

In Medicine Man's mind, his labyrinthine mind, the woman is lover and mother and goddess and daughter. She is the woman leaving his father. She is the sacrifice to save. This woman is the well spring of lust and the first hint of his vulnerability. She represents his true exposure and must be protected. Surely, the sun shines just for her. And he imagines that the silver, white moon rises, and the wind must move, just for her, seeking only to sway soft, against her skin. Medicine Man is convinced that this woman will save him. She will be the last scratched for, clawed for, desperate hand hold. She will be that which keeps him from plummeting into the abyss of dark magic and fear and power.

All these visions expand and collapse within him at the speed of emotion and goose bumps. They wash through him like a flash flood shoving detritus before, leaving sloshing dark waves and destruction in their wake. These visions move across his face and his body as tremors and seizures and shaking bones.

Woman moves to him and he clutches her and holds her to himself with desperate strength. She is bent backwards and dwarfed and frightened by his powers and the swirling black sky and the fleeing squirrels. The woman's eyes, before filled with some sort of awe and love, widen with fear. Medicine Man is consumed by hunger and begins to devour her. He is pulling her very soul from her with every breath. She is shrinking and he is growing. His power is like a monstrous wave building, and the woman is tossed and flung about like some hapless broken ship caught in a typhoon. There is a crash, and he is done. The young woman collapses to the forest floor emptied of life and Medicine Man is larger, exultant, a giant force who,

Ha!,

shouts to the sky, so that the new clouds run, dispersed like sheep fleeing a wolf.

Medicine Man feels as tall as the tallest tree. He can smell the far away salty water and is filled with the life force and the newness that rightfully belongs to the young woman. He is momentarily free of the constant questions, a triumphant and full.

When the euphoria ebbs, Medicine Man sees the woman there lifeless. A sickness comes over him. All his twists and tangles revive, so that there is guilt and horror, mingled with a secret sense of rightness and entitlement. Medicine Man feels the self-loathing and the pleasure and the grief and now again, the young woman is mother or lover or daughter and dead. He cannot stand himself in several ways. Disgust and satiation co-exist so that he is at once smug and fulfilled and wretched with a knowing that he is ultimately, irredeemably, vile.

Rushing to the woman's side, Medicine Man waves his hands and leaning forward returns a hint of her breath. She inhales and her chest moves and some flush blooms on her cheek, she will live. The resentment he feels is familiar to him and so, he sighs.

***

She lies on the soft green ground. Tiny blue flowers are sprinkled around her like stars in a green-brown sky. The young woman breathes rapid and shallow, then slower and deepening. She flutters her eyelids and wakes.

The young woman is beautiful in her wan-ness. Pale and fearful she stares up at Medicine Man with frightened eyes and she flinches from his touch. She sees in him the boy and the monster and the collision that creates such a dangerous beast. He has need like a boy, security, nurturing, safety, and some challenge but, he loathes the need in himself and he reviles his goodness as weakness. It is weakness that scares Medicine Man more than anything.

She sees the dark, swirling lines on his body, with their ever-changing shapes. She watches the coloring in Medicine Man's eyes with their shifting and changing lights that describe, in turn, a frightened teen and a powerful wizard. This terrible combination of frightened boy and colossal power is an aberration, an insult to good sense and the young woman knows she must kill this creature before he kills her and everyone else in the village. And so, reaching within, to some inner core, she summons a small smile.

Medicine Man sees her small frailty and hates her so thoroughly that he feels happy again and so helps her to her feet and spins his lie of a foolish girl going so deeply into the throes of passion that she had passed out. He hides from himself more than from her. He is a devil, a demon, an evil man.

Together the couple stands, each with false face and they break from this place and move towards the village. It is a sick feeling that young woman has, topped with a knowing that the Medicine Man must die.

It is dawning realization Medicine Man has, that he is so much more than these people can ever comprehend and he feels gracious and large and brings them strong medicines and is contemptuous of all peoples and thinks nothing of the grass and the tree and the squirrel or bird.

Man and Woman

Energy

Just before a storm arrives, coastal air becomes heavy, laden with salt and rain, pressure dropping down and down to low and sucking the clouds in, swirling and thickening and grey and dark and black. Winds will be whipping the tops off the waves, the rolling waves, dark and deep and rolling as if running and perpetrating an all-wave assault on the shoreline, angry and anxious to reclaim the land that was once submerged, dark, deep and silent from the long journey from wherever waves are born.

The trees will sway, and groan and creak and animals hide low and close to the ground. The wild roiling sky will sometimes go silent then and turn an ominous green and all will become still. Every living being will hold their breath in anticipation. In a moment, the power will be unleashed and wild and thrashing about wanton as a woman in love, in a fury, a breathless display of energy and power beyond all human comprehension. The storm will come ashore, and giant trees will be whipped and bent like blades of grass on some prairie somewhere east.

On these days, the wizards and the teachers come.

On these days, the Young Woman and her old teacher Raven come.

On these days, the Medicine Man and the ghost of Old Man come.

Power draws them. When the Earth speaks, the natural people, both living and passed, journey to the storm. They come to learn of power and recklessness and pressure dropping to pop the ears. The taste of salt in the air begins many miles inland and salty wind scrubs their skin raw and floods their mouths with water and quickens and freshens and seduces.

The wild ones, the shaman, feel the thrill of all that energy and fly faster with hunger, with abandon, with need. They come to feel small. To witness the immensity of a storm allows these magicians the feeling of being powerless and tossed and awed; and for the duration of these stormy moments, they thrill to be free, free of the responsibility of being the power. Here, the shaman are the beings restored.

Bearing witness to a force beyond what they can control, they all, even Raven and the ghost of Old Man, are filled with wonder, held enthralled and possessed by a reverent feeling, a feeling in the middle of their being that is as charged and potent as the streaks of lightening that fly from the vast and terrible turned sky.

These are the times when Medicine Man appears as a boy again.

The Old Man's ghost stands clinging to his stick, his white hair flashing all around and the hint of a smile upon his face. Man/Boy vibrates with an ecstatic trembling, a shiver bouncing through his frame until he cannot help but take flight. He is immediately tossed, tumbling through the low heavy sky, twisting and turning to avoid collisions, climbing higher, slightly higher, clearing most treetops, brushing against the tops of the tallest, screaming exaltations and Old Man's ghost smiles and remembers and feels his own essence quicken.

These are the times when the Young Woman appears as an angel, translucent and glowing from within. She exists as both creator and resident; joy contained in a bubble of serenity. She is the center and the serene and the storm all at once. Raven, slightly annoyed as usual, struts and scolds and makes sarcastic remarks but he too is thrilled with the ruffle of his feathers, the groaning and moaning of the trees. And though he stays low and close to the giant tree trunks that keep him safe; he too bounces up and down, so overwhelmed with exhilaration that even he cannot hide his glee.

Young Woman stands and the winds and the rains part around her. They flow over and by, like the dark rolling waves slice around the large rocks, spraying high, dashing themselves against the giants over and over. The waves never care if the rocks ever move. They are only glad to have a place to crash, to express their power, to display the pent-up color and froth of their long grey journey. And Young Woman serene, smiles and radiates ...love. She holds a different sort of reverence than any of the others here. Hers is not awe and thrill and fear-tinged exhilaration, rather it is a profound peace. For the Young Woman the storm is a step across some craggy threshold. Carried aloft on the gusting winds she enters her very own cathedral, with the sky as ceiling and earth as floor, mountainous buttresses and windows framed with cloud. When the storm comes, Young Woman does not feel small, she feels infinite.

So, it is no wonder, that when the Man/ Boy sees, he sees a Young Woman standing, arms lifted, upholding the crazed and turbulent sky. Her hands turn and point, shape and curve. She is a conductor coaxing more here, less there, and the dancing streaks of lightening obey and the claps of thunder follow. The Young Woman does not generate the powerful storm but surfs its waves, carving lines that match those tattooed on the Old Man's skin, only white as the light bouncing off a daisy's petal.

It seems that the storm is a generous hymn, a symphony played just for her, at her bequest and under her direction. And the Man/Boy feels...the power of her song and his own vulnerability and a deep desire to fall at the Young Woman's feet and kiss her knees. And in this feeling of losing himself to another and becoming touchable, he recoils and a sneering, mean fear grips him entire. Fundamental cruelty fills his arms and thighs and his chest bulges with the energy of hate.

Man is confused as to where to point and ravage. Should he hate his weakness or the one who elicits the longing to rest, to fall, to surrender unto and float, immersed and safe.

Safe,

is the word which sends him violently spinning, screeching and clawing at his own flesh. Filled with self-loathing Man returns to the front, the edge of the weather and collects to himself the powers of the storm, neither noticing, nor caring, about the terrible toll this imposes on his soul. He does not see that with each new infusion of power he is becoming more and more difficult to look at.

Filled and full, holding as much power as he can contain, Man has become ugly. His skin is stretched into a monstrous mask. His bones have been broken and bent, curved and twisted into odd shapes. Man has become hard to look at for all but the Old Man's ghost. He tries to move the clouds. He tries to redirect the wind, but the storm only laughs in his face. The Man is still weak when compared to the Woman and his fear is rising.

Man's fear is rising, and he has fallen. He lays on the hardpacked wet sand, broken at his keel, washed ashore as any wreck, tossed by any storm.

The Old Man's ghost has watched and measured and still believing he can redirect the Man, he approaches. The old man is ephemeral and faint. He is noiseless and leaves no footprint. He is full of concern. He sees that Man has become hideous, a physical manifestation of the fear that is churning and coiling through his mind like a serpent. Man sees himself reflected in the old ghost's eyes and cannot tolerate neither his own visage, nor the the compassion shining forth. In this moment, the Old Man is unmasked and his love for the boy shines. The Old Ghost's true face at last revealed and he is kindness.

Possessed by a hatred that consumes all reason, fueled by the power of his shame, Man unleashes his fury and ends the Old Man for once and forever. Man has been seized and consumed by fear. Any remaining vestige of humanity is buried so deep as to be gone altogether. He picks himself up from the sand and shakes himself off. Man considers the old ghost gone, shrugs, smirks and moves. He knows where to go.

Death in the Village

Man's fear is rising. He travels fast to his home. His wife is there. Surely, she will soothe and temper this shrieking sharp pain that burns deep in his chest.

Returning to spend his hatred and fear upon his young girl wife, Man begins killing her over and over. With each kiss, with each ghastly embrace, he draws the life from her until she fades and falls dead. Each time resurrecting her, begging her for forgiveness, slyly watching as a demon trickster, watching to see if he can turn the young woman's innate sense of compassion and forgiveness against her.

Driving his doubt knife deep, Man works to set his wife against herself. Her love is sustenance for the monster Man has become. She sees that it is her own love that is growing him, sustaining him and she hardens her heart to withhold, and this is a murderous thing to her own being. By nature, she is kind, compassionate and loving, and so she is at war with her very self. Man feeds on her struggle.

When she loves him? He feasts. When she fears him and cannot summon compassion, she is internally ripping herself apart and the Man feeds on this pain, too.

Man takes his wife into the woods and murders her over and over, drawing the life force from her and taking it into himself. She dies over and over and over, and he is losing his sadness's. Those small moments, when witnessing the results of his behavior used to create some feeling, some sliver of regret, are fading. Like smoke dispersing, they are disappearing into the complete lack of light, the dark night of the creature he is becoming, has become.

The Man's young wife is recovering less and less. He is leaving her hurt and alone, deep in the forest. He performs his resurrections and casually walks away, leaving her to stumble back to the village by herself. Man often laughs without reason, some secret humor inside him seeks any last bit of humanity left inside him, seeking and searching and wiping goodness-es from existence until one day he is just too far gone to remember to resurrect his wife. He leaves his young bride there, crumpled and wadded up on the forest floor, all the life has been pulled from her and she is gone.

Returning to the village he sees the frightened eyes searching behind him, hoping. And he has a small flash and turns and poisons the air with magic words which choke and blind and leave all writhing on the ground in the throes of leaving and the Bad Man watches and feels nothing. Not even the past joy of watching life leave can touch the void he is becoming, would be completely, if not for one last, nagging need. He will find the storm Woman again and erase her, take for himself all her life. And when he does leave her lifeless and drained body, laying empty on the cold beach, he will have left his very last weakness laying there beside her.

***

Day after day, Bad Man exists in his own spinning hate. And going only inward, he spirals into himself. Forgetting to eat or bathe or move, he is become a pale, emaciated, dirty tangled creature with claws. The shapes carved into his body take more and more of any space and consume more and more of any mind and overlapping they become confusing, so that even the stench of the corpses he lives with does not penetrate his awareness.

Sometimes Bad Man sees his father laying there on the ground with his severed spinal cord, helpless to prevent any violence being visited upon his wife and child. Bad Man sees again the hopelessness, the despair on his father's face as he looks not towards Mother but towards son. And in the Bad Man's own black rage, ashes sometimes fall from the grey sky, drifting to the ground as snowflakes and reminding him of his night under the tree in the cold snow grave, feeling his mother walk away.

Someday, some time.

The Bad Man resolves to find her and to find him and make them into pain.

Weeks go and go, and the air is heavy pregnant again. Bad Man knows the storm is coming and that the storm Woman will be there. He is interested in something outside himself for the first time in a very long time and he feels in his center that he will consume this woman. The thought lifts him to his feet and from his broken reverie, he smells himself even more overpowering than the mostly gone corpses of the villagers. He sees his hands dry, bony, and claw like and so he walks haltingly to the small lake and eases himself down into the icy waters, brown with color from the fallen leaves. Some shock, some chill sends a shiver up his spine and he is staring straight at himself as a child, falling, falling for the girl now dead and dried.

Bad Man remembers and allows feeling to fill him up until he is ripe as fruit, his skin stretched taut and his heart stretched and the vulnerability of need of want, and he shakes himself visibly and drops under the surface to scrub the filth off him. Suspended there he listens to the rush of blood through his veins and the puh-pumping of his heart. Gazing up he sees the rippling shiny mirror mercury surface and watches as it seems so far away. This cold is a different cold, and he shudders and surfaces, breaking through the skin of the water and stands gasping for breath, rolls his shoulders back and walks slowly to the shallows and up and onto the bank. Time to go.

Storm arrives

All the nations lay down and press themselves close to the earth. They feel the dirt scrub rough and warm against their cheeks and the grasses tickle their noses. They spread palms wide and scratch and seek purchase and firm connection with the ground. All has fallen quiet.

The sky has turned green and there is a still, silent, heavy weight pause, like just after you leap from a tall craggy cliff, just before gravity has taken hold, not flying, not falling... suspended, timeless.

There is only a moment, a minute before the earth will inhale and gather Her lungs full of air, air then expelled and gusting forth with such wild freedom that clothing will be ripped and torn from backs. Animals will forget to breathe and only close their eyes waiting, waiting for this madness to pass.

Lightening streaks the sky and boom after booming low bass, comes rolling thunder, vibrating the very soul, the all, the everything. Wind goes whipping with such frenzy and abandon that even Trees are flung about in some manic dance. Air thick, throbbing, pulsing with energy and power, is a thrashing pent-up scream of unrequited want, need and lust. Desperate for connection, left wanting too long, the charged Earth must be relieved in an unfettered, unconstrained explosion of reckless abandon and passion.

And Bad Man is coming.

And the storm Woman is coming.

Bad Man feels the surging, the buffeting wind in waves, pounding, provoking, and escalating his essence, filling his heart, his chest, his face no... visage, with a hate so black that his eyes change, changing, pupil dilating until there is nothing but black and the dancing of the shapes, the liquid lines moving and aligning. He is fully become a monstrous being.

Flashing forward, trailing his wake of sickness so vile that grasses brown and birds fall from shelter and are tossed through the air, helpless and stunned. He is growing.

Woman hurries. Her mouth is dry, her lips swollen and her heart pounds like an insistent drum. She feels a down low wetness and a hunger that blooms like a flower reaching out to hold the sun. There is an unpracticed urgency in her travel and while she maintains the pleasantries, they are all a bit vague, amorphous, and undefined. She finds it hard to see over the bright shining hardness of the need that is consuming her, spreading from belly to chest to limbs and brain. She would be confused but for the fact that she is not thinking at all, only flying forward on instinct.

The freshness of the storm, the wind and electrified air are blushing Woman's cheeks and narrowing her eyes and she moves uncharacteristically straight-line, knowing exactly where she must be.

Drawn towards one another inexorably, it is like night touches day. Bad Man and Woman have to happen.

There is a space, a clearing, a meadow. It sits with a view of the vast rolling ocean and its grey waves with their foamy white tops. There is a cliff face, where rocks have tumbled down to litter a small, dark sand beach. The ground up above the cliff is sandy too, with low tangled trees and head high grasses. Back a bit more the tall pines reach, reaching up so high that it hurts the neck to stare at their tops, and then there is the meadow. All out of place in this ocean side scape it has low brown grasses as soft as satin and is dotted here and there with close to the ground blossoms of bright yellow, sky blue and an impossible white. The grasses here are pressed down, turned on their sides soft, though not by rain. Here only a few raindrops fall, though it is clear to see the downpour all around and up above. Here in the meadow the rain falls so soft that the ground is not really wet. The rain here, instead of acting as curtain, behaves like some strange glass that sharpens and illuminates and brings all objects near and crystal clear. The edge of each section of bark, on each giant rusty Tree, each deeply green pine needle and each brushy branch end, stand in sharp focus. The sounds of the storm are howl and moan, growing and breaking and thrashing until it is only the coyote's song sung a hundred times louder, a thousand times more plain, magnified and sharpened by the soft, soft rain.

Here, in this meadow, Bad Man and Woman alight and stare across, feeling their faces squirm and shift, feeling their own muscles ripple and swell. The lines on Bad Man's body lift away from his skin and spin out to the center of the meadow. Woman's own lines move to meet, and at once the power hieroglyphics collide. There is a primitive combat filled with deadly intent. There is a chaotic spinning, thrusting grasping seeking to dominate and bear down to the earth and shake the life from the other, amongst the strange flying forms, those electric swooshing symbols of power. And while they engage, the humans stand nude.

He is young after all, skin smooth, tautly drawn, lithe and lean and swift and dangerous in the healthy animal way of his kind.

She is Woman with all the strength and will and roundnesses here, and flat places there. Her shape IS the shape of enduring and fertility and life and tempest.

Woman smiles a small greedy smile and feels how her body has filled and fattened, plumped and become the center, the single source of gravity pulling him inescapably to her, and he thinks, he really believes, believes that he is in charge. Only when he touches her electric skin, only too late, does Bad Man realize that he has been caught, captured and bound and is wholly hers for the sake of life.

He wraps her in his brown storm wind arms and kisses drops of rain from her lowered eyelids and their hair entwines and their legs entwine. There is the brilliant life light shining forth and being swallowed up. And there is hunger and need, breath and beat, push and pull.

A crushing merge and two are one. The high winds sob in exaltation, and sincerely the Bad Man and the Woman are now the origins, yang and yin, source and end. Consuming one another as an avalanche, a flashing fire, unleashing every meaningful power, demolishing every natural and unnatural law, claiming unfamiliar territory, new space, and there is crescendo after crescendo until falling spent upon their backs they gaze blankly up into the clouds and the rain comes down and washing, washes away the heat or they might have burned or set fire at the very least. So cooling lips de-flame and on their skin, piloerection and goosebumps smooth.

All tumbled together with grass for a bed, and flower for a pillow, the two inhabit a separate place, a bubble created via the intensity of their lovemaking. And the storm swirls round.

Bad Man feels the cooling drops falling upon his face, they strike and splash and slide down and off and tickle his ears. It is possible that tears are mingling in and amongst the rain drops. There is some strange and unwelcome sensation that he has, to be seen and known and accepted. Bad Man feels his anger empty and powerless. Who is he if not some vile, hate filled creature? And in the stirrings of connection and attachment deep within he feels fear. These feelings lead to pain and rage and hatred, and darkness is far superior to fear, as far as feelings go.

Glancing sideways he sees the Woman laying on her back, eyes closed and a slight curve on her lips indicating a happy relaxation. The Bad Man shudders and feels the pangs of fear grow larger and louder.

Woman sighs and reaches a hand softly over and places it on the Bad Man's chest, she feels his heart thudding anxiety, and sends warming, calming, quieting energy through her hand and into his center.

Bad Man, shudders even harder, his body spasming with the strength and the newness of these unfamiliar sensations. Small sounds burst through his lips and escape into the atmosphere, and he is shocked at the betrayal of his very own body and throat.

He tries to rise, to climb to his feet in defiance of these sweet vulnerabilities and is unable. Chained here, riveted, anchored, held prisoner by his hunger and need for this human touch and warmth, he curses and chuckles and twists and turns in his mind, but he does not rise, he does not stand up, only moves closer to the Woman and that nurturing femininity that he so clearly craves.

Slowly his heart rate subsides, slows, eases until he is almost relaxed. Only in his innermost place is there still that taut stretched nervousness, strung so tightly that it may snap at any moment. The Bad Man feels almost drowsy and allows himself a contented sigh and sinks further into the earth.

Woman feels his slow surrender and smiles even more tenderly than before. She herself is sated, the bright edged hunger gone and, in its place, a lazy, sensual, lush sense of contentment. All is well.

As the sounds of the storm penetrate her awareness, she stirs a bit and moves closer to the man, seeking closeness and warmth like any animal does in times of terrible weather, terrible natural forces and energies being flung and splashing all about. The man stiffens in momentary resistance and she jostles him gently and he relents, relaxes, and falls ever farther into the Woman. And soon they will make love again, here under the dark swollen clouds and the fat falling drops, here and here and here.

The soft grasses caress and the petals delicate touch and the sigh and the filling and full and the fattened lips brushing teasing and the pressing and opening and softer than before because now is not need, it is wanting, and then that is all the more delicious. And the Man is moving, and Woman is moving and claiming authority now, and the Man is falling into some foreign place, some alien feeling of ease, and he forgets to let his eyes dart around, and he forgets to stoke his cynicism and bitterness and he falls, falls as if from some great height, stomach spinning away from him and heart filling and expanding. He feels himself giving something to this woman that he did not even know he had. And he looks up into her eyes, into her face and she is looking down at him and everything she does is power of a sort he has never known.

The Man's breath quickens, deepens, becomes as a bellows, in and out and he is not breathing himself. There is some force beyond his ken, some elemental or essential energy that is breathing him. And his body is rolling. And he is swept away and closing his eyes, taken by this wave, these waves and completely gone, he is out of his mind. The breathing thing that is happening to him is happening to his body and to his mind and the undulations of belly and breath become orgasm and pleasure and his entire body is writhing and searching for closer, nearer deeper more merged and as the orgasm has taken him and seconds and minutes go by and his moan begins to rise forth unbidden. The woman hears and her stoicism is cracking. And her rhythm is taking her too and then together they are both gone and one and rising and disintegrating into tiny particles, diffuse, intermingled and are they people or gods or plants or sky? Tis impossible to know and those are thoughts and words which are far to pale too communicate the bliss, the ecstasy the euphoria...these are not quite right because it is not a state the two experience, it is something they become. And there they remain for some moments, some minutes, some hour until Woman leans forward and slides off to the side and Man is empty and spent, and all that remains of him are the lingering feelings of Woman and her original energy.

The fierce storm roiling in an unleashing of all the power of nature, slows and sighs into calm as Woman inhales and fills up and exhales and falls into slumber.

Man rolls onto his side and propping himself on his elbow gazes without restrain upon her face. He marvels at the smooth, calm, beauty there, where moments ago lay unbridled passion and power.

It is hard to say what emotions course through him, but his face ripples and writhes, shifts and twists as some internal debate takes place. Having learned the perils of vulnerability, having experienced the afterglow of cruelty and murder, Man lies here with all his warped desperation and fear clashing with this new feeling of safety, of finally, of rest and acceptance.

Bad Man physically softens and melts lower to the earth, he shivers and feels chilly and hungry and sleepy all at the same time. As his eyelids flutter shut and he sighs into sleep, he feels the glimmer of some new thing, some opening, some small love.

Woman rests her hand lightly in his and turns away from him to snuggle back into his warmth and to feel this connecting rest. They sleep.

The storm rages on all around until spent and then moves on, but with much less power.

When Woman wakes, she glances to the Man. She feels some affection, some kindnesses in her center and she smiles and Man, opening his eyes, sees her smile and falls further.

She stands. Her wind soft hair frames her glowing face, and she looks deeply into the Man's eyes and sends warmth and gratitude and says her goodbyes. Man does not move, watching in wonder as she gathers herself, her lines are returned upon her body and the shapes are softer and more maternal and happier and his lines have returned, and they too are softer and positioned differently, nothing noticeable really, just a blurring and rounding. Woman waves her hand across the air and pushes towards the man and he feels this caress and feels the falling and Woman has turned and rising, walking, moving, leaving, goes.

Man tries to stand and makes it to his knees, where sitting baffled, he watches her back, her long flowing hair and her warm, warm legs slicing through the golden grasses until she has reached the edge of the bubble and is gone.

His head tilts forward, and he stares down at his hands, brown and clean. It is as if he has never seen them before, never known these foreign far away appendages could process so much moon softness strength of a sort he had never contemplated or heard of from the Old Man. The very ridges on the tips of his fingers feel thicker, more pronounced. And he longs even now for the feel of them dragging across her soft invitational skin, the way the swirls and circles would collect her shine, her radiance, the emanating essence of her. And for a moment he feels the air filtered through her constitution and the viscosity of it, the golden sweet honey of it is squeezing his heart and cracking it open. And there, he recalls her liquid eyes, whites and browns and golden flecks, reflecting back a vision of himself as he had never before considered.

Shaking his head to clear this madness Man rises to his feet and stretches. He is hungry.

After Storm Woman

The storm has eased. Winds still deliver the occasional gust, but altogether the feel is manageable. The before driving rain is now only a clean evaporating smell and droplets of water clinging to, slipping down and falling down, from tree branches, needles and leaves. The electric green thinness of the air before the storm has given way to a clean, damp, smell and a relaxed vibration of assessment. The animal nations are checking in on their homes and setting about the business of life.

Woman is satiated, satisfied and that craving mad hunger from before is gone, replaced by a small rueful smile and a relaxed swinging of her arms. She swirls and skims about in the newly washed forest, swimming, dancing and skipping south. She is heading towards home and she is in no hurry and feels comfortable everywhere and is accompanied by many. Even the Trees bid her good journey and reach forth to lightly brush her skin and her hair. Woman smiles and sings along with the birds and bids good mornings and good days to the deer and the rabbit and the fox.

It is only weeks later that she first begins to notice an unusual sensation. She is nauseous in the morning and is careful with food. There is some new stirring in her tummy, and she is aware that a life is begun inside of her. Woman awakens to this knowing and a secret smile curls her lips.

Well now. This was unexpected.

And she hurries a little bit as she moves ever south, heading to home. Now there is reason to move, purpose in her step. Soon she must begin preparations for the oncoming upheavals.

She will be a Mother.

Woman's cheeks flush red with the knowledge and the awakening ideas of impending parenthood. She never considers the Man in dogged pursuit; he was only a moment and the moment is gone and now never crosses her mind.

Once home, back in her meadow, near the icy stream she stops and sits and marvels. The birds have come to rest with her, the grasses have bent her way and Woman plots her new life. With one hand on her tummy, not yet rounding out, she gazes out to the rippling waters and the rising land and the steady mountains.

Woman considers all the mothers and the one Mother. She savors this sense of wonder tinged with fear and flavored with a deep satisfaction. She is ready and a humming low in her throat signals contentment.

Woman goes about the business of gathering, making ready foodstuffs and collecting firewood. She will need extra blankets and sitting one evening near the glowing fire and watching the reflected flames flicker on the still, glassy water, she sings the songs of a soon to be mother and the coyotes join in and round and round are the animal nations. Their eyes glow red and they join Woman in song. There is a peace and a resoluteness to all that are here.

The master engineers of the animal nations come, and the right trees are felled and stacked and pulled and taking shape is a new lodge, a new home built for the two. The bird families are pitching in and filling all the smaller gaps, the spaces between branches. Where they find their materials is as mysterious as ever, but in short order there is a dry and comfortable new living space built. The insides are being lined with furs and shaped and tortoises, pushing and placing ancestor rocks, have created the perfect stone pit. There are bunks for sleeping and shelves holding containers and all manner of necessities. Woman chatters happily with all of those working and at the same time is completely absorbed in her own project. She is weaving a basket of sorts, with handles and straps and clearly it is for carrying or rocking or protecting baby.

Each day Woman feels the growing child dance in her belly and each day she feels a growing maternal sense of responsibility and love. Even when she wanders barefoot down to the stream and steps into its gently moving shallows her attention is largely focused inwards, hands on her belly as if already holding the tiny being growing there.

When one morning she looks up and sees the Man there she is surprised but not startled. He has come, and she has more curiosity than anything else. Why is he here? How will he respond to her new condition? Her swelling belly makes it very clear that a child is growing inside her.

The Man stands just clear of the tree line. He is stunned into stillness, his body motionless, his eyes gone wide. He is filled with some alien feeling, some mixture of trepidation and pride and worry and weight.

He looks good. The journey has been good to the Man. He is lean and strong. His skin glows healthy with the fading, almost gone marks of magic, of wizardry and power. His hair hangs long. He is relaxed and tall.

Woman stands, water streaming over her feet like a soothing massage and stares at the man. Her hand goes to her belly as if to reassure. This is an unexpected complication. She continues to stare evenly, and the Man begins to collect himself. He is at turns embarrassed, fascinated, shocked and intrigued. The Woman is clearly pregnant.

Stupidly he searches around looking for her husband or lover, whomever has put her in this condition must surely be nearby and Bad Man scowls, roughs his face with his palms and looks behind him as if unsure whether to run away or stride forward. He has been made a fool by this Woman and he considers that she must pay dearly, the old snake of hate slithers in his guts, raising its head and filling his arms with power, and his mind with anger.

Bad Man raises his hands parallel to the earth and exudes his killing will through his palms and down towards the earth, but it is too little, and he sees only a slight browning of the grass and his countenance goes from cold to confused and he brings to bear his powers and nothing. And in his center a tiny piece of ice forms and takes the center of what had been a growing core of warmth and wonder. He is frightened.

Woman sees his changing face, his brown healthy body and flashing black eyes. She watches as he levels his hands towards the earth and pulses them in small circular movements as if testing the density of the air between his palms and the great mother. She watches as he turns his gaze downwards, his head drooping, dropping in defeat or acceptance or contemplation and she feels the stirring life within. With a small swirl of her hand a slight breeze gusts towards the Man and rocks him forward enough so that he peers up under lowered brow. He sees her there and she is beauty, not beautiful but beauty itself and glowing with the light of two lives and radiating the nurturing rich thick maternal. The Man is drawn to this power and is at the same time sprouting within himself a self-loathing of sorts, he is after all weak and still longs for what he himself never had. This turning in, this withdrawing and shrinking smaller has pulled the Woman towards him in compassion and she is sending waves of connecting energy and the Man and the Woman are drawing nearer and his hand is on his knife and her hand is on her belly and she is smiling sweetly, shyly but with power and he is smiling, and it is with the thought of her red blood warming and coating his hands as he slides the knife deep.

Woman comes to some decision and flows to the Man and she does not hear any warning from any person or people or nation. And the opening and the smile on her face do not change the Man's mind, only confuse him for a moment, two moments, long enough for Woman to reach him and stop, standing in front of him, looking up at him with a vulnerability and an asking. And reaching out to touch his hand and his cheek and she understands only that he is in shock and so is gentle and pulls his hand to her belly and smiles.

Dimly, so tiny and far away that it is almost imperceptible, a tiny glimmer of a thought enters Man's mind that he may be wrong, that all is not what he thinks and there is a great war within him between insecurity and hope. He dares not believe in this Woman, in this other, and yet he almost does and he is shaking uncontrollably and sick and his head is full of fog and cloud and cotton and he cannot hear anything but the thrumming in his ears, the thunder thumping of his heart. The glimmer of thought is broadening and growing and is a sliver, a wedge. Man is carrying in his belly the beginnings of awareness.

Man collapses to his knees and is weeping aloud. He places his cheek on Woman's belly. She strokes his hair and murmurs soft consolations and comforts.

What now, what now.

Woman pulls Man to his feet and looks into his face, caresses his cheek and gently smiles.

After Storm Man

It is weeks gone since Man and Woman lay together and still the sensation of that day lies on his skin like perspiration, shiny, glistening, sticky and thin. Man goes through his days in a happy confusion, his body grows stronger and more chiseled. He stands taller and sees farther through clearer eyes, steady, bereft of the twitchy sullenness of before.

Man's legs feel like powerful springs and his shoulders have broadened and animals no longer flee before him. He hums under his breath and wanders forward in no particular hurry, stopping often to stare far away and out. He does not return to the haunted village where death hangs heavy and low in the air, a terrible fog cloaking, consuming and blurring all. The smell there is repulsive to him now and so he moves steadily south, though he is unaware of his decision to do so.

Each day Man rises with the sun. He likes to sit quietly and watch the sun come up while the birds sing in the new day. Man searches and finds the streams, the rivers, the dammed ponds where beaver live and shivering, makes his way naked down to water's edge. He moves in an unhurried way, singing, chanting and laughing quietly at himself. Easing himself into the frigid highland waters he delights in the fiery burning feel of the chill water moving up his skin inch by inch and step by step until he finally plunges fully under.

And after each immersion the Man emerges gasping and laughing and leaping skyward with great splashes and spray, shouting and shuddering. Man is cleansing himself. Unconsciously he seeks out fresh, cold waters to bathe and the lushest green grasses to lay on while the sunlight dries and warms his skin. He watches clouds float overhead and marvels as they shift and turn, disappear, reappear, and morph into one vision after another.

Content to be a human animal, Man eats when he is hungry, sleeps when he is tired and walks with no hurry, no immediate purpose, and no anger. If there is some new motivating force it is wonder, as the scales fall from his eyes and the cloudiness clears from his lungs.

One day he feels a rumbling low beat rising up from the ground. It is as if the earth itself were breathing. He strides faster then, swinging his arms and lengthening his steps until he crests a low ridge and stops. Here Man sits and watches for two entire days as a herd of great buffalo mosey by, so close he can smell their raw power. The shadows of the forest are hard to see into from this bright shiny place. Here in the glaring daylight brightness, Man's eyes have changed, and he can no longer penetrate the distant dark veil. And besides, it is cold there and warm here and Man is content. He is going in search of the Woman.

Turning his awareness in her direction, he experiences for the first time in many, many years an uncertainty. Man is unable to send himself out and up and away and searching. The clouds, once his playmates, remain high up and out of his reach. Man can no longer fly. He gives an unruffled shake of his head, experiences a slight confusion and

no matter he smiles,

no matter.

The sun is warm on his shoulders and the air is clean, light and clear. Striding forward in long, easy, rolling steps, Man feels the earth soft under his feet. He wakes and walks and breathes. The good air moves into and then out of him, blurring and dissolving any distinction, any separation. Slowly, Man is becoming clean, his fear and pain cannot hold at bay the changing, dancing, laughing power of moving on foot through the great, green forests.

Man smiles at the sky and pauses to lick the occasional flower because they seem so soft and full of color and life. And why wouldn't they taste wonderful? Unnoticed, unremarked, Man's magical powers are fading, fading to almost gone, replaced by an awe and an immediate sort of immersion in the here and now. The smell of pine, mixed with the slight scent of the faraway salty ocean and the not so far away musty wild bear smell are intoxicating and he does not miss his stranger, uglier, more disengaging talents.

These days when an animal offers itself for food it is not with rolling eyes, frothing breath and trembling legs. The squirrel, the rabbit and the golden speckled trout fish offer themselves more willingly, sensing no devil here, no darkness. Man has become near transparent; he smells of grasses and trees and soft breezes. As he has crossed over high places his old markings have faded, the burning in the center of his mind has eased and the dark cold death that has been his wake has gone. Man travels as a natural person, leaving earth as he finds it, green, brown, blue, red and orange, bright and alive.

Together

Woman is fascinated by the life growing within her. Often, she stands gazing off into space while resting her hands on her tummy.

What child will come? Will she be quick and beautiful, or will he be a wizard or a hunter? Or maybe SHE will be a wizard or a hunter and HE, beautiful and quick.

***

Woman is not in the here place, instead she floats somewhere in the in-between. Not between dimensions, but between the inside and the out. Woman works to prepare a place for baby while at the same time a part of her consciousness is always with the child, already loving, feeding and teaching and connecting with the being inside her. It has been many weeks since she travelled as she was taught, and she only thinks of it in passing and they are fond thoughts, but not relevant to the moment; she is growing a baby and it requires all of her.

***

Man is connecting with the animals and the birds. He had forgotten or perhaps never known, how cheerful and hardworking the nations are in general. He is learning from the beaver how to build and learning from the fish patience. He spends hours each day watching the hawk spiral overhead before plunging down and killing her meal. He hears clearly the conversation between all the nations, and he is awed into stillness. In the mornings, Man wakes to look at Woman. He watches her sleeping and hears her murmuring sounds of comfort and her teachings to the child growing in her belly, his child. Most mornings Man steals away, outside before the sun comes up. In the still of dawn, he sits and wonders at the clean clear skies and rubs his arms to vanquish the morning chill.

It is as the sun comes up and he has finished his morning bath and swim, while he is sitting in the earliest low rays of warmth to dry, that he finally notices the shapes, the markings on his skin, have faded and are almost gone. He stares dumbly for a very long time, mind empty of anything serious, only a mild curiosity exists there. He lifts his hand before his face and turning it this way and that, marvels at his own appearance. He is brown and full of water and life, his skin glows with health. Reaching up, his long dark hair feels strong and vital, and he feels the strength of cleanliness and love, full in his body. There is barely a trace of power, only a thin trace of darkness buried so far down and away that Man is not moved by it at all, only peripherally aware that it hides, weak and childish somewhere deep inside.

He presses his hand out over the grasses and wills the green, silver gold blades to move and they barely lean, it may even be that it was only the slightest morning breeze that created any movement at all. Man is pondering this transformation and, while it is fragile, there is a sort of acceptance and even happiness about his new beingness.

Woman steps out from the shelter and the flap falls closed and she stands in the first morning sun naked and golden and round and looks at Man questioning. He rises. He rises and walks over to her placing a gentle hand on her belly and her neck and leaning in close whispers love words and connecting reassuring words. And when she is ready, he helps

Woman walk down the dewy grass slope and navigate her way over the bank and down into the icy waters of the stream.

Man notices the slight luminescence of her markings, her powers; and feels only curious. And she eases deeper into the crisp cold wetness.

In the evening, in the warm glow of the shelter fire, with the thick smells of herbs and foods and home and hearth and love and family, the Woman's eyes open wide, and she clutches her belly and there is a slight wincing then a slow smiling and she knows it is now.

Man awakens, and she caresses his cheek. She smoothes his hair, soothes his worry and nudges him out, outside. In the firelight, he stands and looks full upon her, and he feels some shifting turning displacement and his heart is full to burst. Between Man and Woman is a wonder, a fierce, fierce tenderness and need. He ducks under the flap and out, to stand full in the light of the moon. Raising his arms, his palms to the sky, Man leans back and begins to sing the song, the songs of birthing and first fathers and banishment of fears.

He sings the songs and prayers for strength and wisdom and patience and above all to not be turned by the fear that every single parent who ever was, knows deep. Man knows, that when you become a parent there comes a vulnerability. There is pride and fatigue. There is a profound joy that issues forth from such a singular source, that should any harm befall this source, father or mother can be robbed of their very soul. Man has seen that, there are pains so terrible that they pull and tug and extract the essential foundational piece from a parent's very being and leave naught behind but a husk, an empty ghost person who wanders and would forget to breathe were it possible.

And so, Man sings louder to the sky, the stars, and his voice is strengthening and finding the rhythm and pulse. All round the nations look to their own and marvel.

***

Woman experiences a very different sort of shifting. There is a gathering of all her scattered parts, a drawing together and coalescing into some strength beyond the ken of men, a power that will sustain through all hardship, any deluge, all droughts. As a mother, Woman will hunger, go days without sleep, carry on while deathly ill or mortally wounded. Woman is becoming a new force of nature and there is a certain gravitational field that comes with this singular steel.

Light as a feather, delicate as brand-new life, she lets the air move out through pursed lips. There are beads of sweat on her brow, and above her lips. The drops sparkle and flash and lay on her skin pregnant themselves, ready to fall and splash and become for a moment and then return to the earth. Dark hair hangs straight and heavy and light flows amongst the strands like a river as she turns restlessly, first one way then another.

There is the flickering light, the tongues of flame, the swirl of some dense air moving in concentric circling waves, and she is being breathed and it is an old thing, in place since the beginning and this instinct has taken over and for once Woman feels small in the face of some magic. She knows, as all those before her have known, that it is time and she pushes once and again and small cries escape her mouth, her heart. Her eyes are closed in concentration and the primal play twists and turns, first the resting then the terrific cramping and the feeling of fever and lost in the swirling moments of separation and sundering. Her shapes and symbols glow wildly bright and there is heat enough to smell her singed skin. Woman sings loud and clear and then pain muffles her voice again, until...on the very next push, baby girl is out and in her mother's arms, and crying out her emerging song.

Man stops his singing and hears his heart swoosh out and away and into the tiny life inside the shelter, resting brand new in Woman's arms and he knows. Man knows, he is mortal and naked and without magic. The terrible vulnerability of it frightens him and he feels weak, weaker than when he was buried in the snow, weaker than when he fell in love with the girl from the village, weaker even than when he lay with Woman in the storm sheltered meadow.

Man does not know the strength of the mother.

Man knows the vulnerability of the father.

The buffalo pause, the Raven is for once silent and the trees go silent and only sway, with their heads in the clouds, and for just this moment. It is one moment only, passing like some melancholic spiritual euphoria that burns so bright that it is consumed and then gone, turned to ash.

Man sits in front of the flap and sighs. He will sit here and guard this portal until asked otherwise. This is how it is. This is how is has always been.

***

Woman, her face now Mother's, is made more beautiful by the severity of her love. There are glints of happiness and freckles of satisfaction and for a second when the baby does latch and eat, something ancient and forever. Woman/Mother is Earth and nurture and more fierce than winter.

On the third day Woman takes fresh water from the basin and washes the child and washes herself and composes herself, allowing for the first-time thoughts of Man and how she must be careful not to frighten him.

She does ask Man,

Open the flap.

And he turns from his place and rises to his feet, feeling the days in his back and the cold in his knees and not minding at all. He will see his child. He will know his child and he will join with Woman and this tiny bit of ice growing in his stomach will surely melt and relent and he will feel summer again.

Lifting the flap out and up, Man extends his hand as to assist Woman and child. She is a new being and she is a new being. There are two. And Man is momentarily non-plussed. Apprehension, pride, aloofness and fascination all war with one another, and he is stiff legged and side eyes and haughty and solicitous all in one, and the scattering of his intentions are confusing him, and he flushes and feels the tightening skin on his face as he is embarrassed. Still, the brief snatches of time, during which, he is able to look full upon his daughter's face, he feels some stillness, some shifting, something right and a correctness.

His baby girl is marked.

The lights move on her newborn skin and her eyes are vague and old.

Woman/Mother stands and allows, she has had three days to come back into this body, this time and this new situation and she is asking man to accelerate this to minutes or moments. She watches from beneath her lashes and sees Man fumble and grasp, discard and then finally leave uncertainty and confusion and open a place for acceptance, and she moves to him and stands under him and close. There is a special way, a woman way, it places her close and under, and is she his root? Or is he her shelter? There is no defining this relationship, only a living expression of partnership, with each bringing their primal parts to bear. And in this close moment, a contract is made, and both are free to be even more themselves than ever before.

***

Man is filled with a new desire to please the Woman/Mother, to protect her and to guard the new baby girl and hold the perimeter safe even while mystified by the center. He will never understand her and never not be helplessly in love with her. She is a mystery as un-fathomable as an ocean, as ephemeral and captivating as the wolf nation's song.

And Woman/Mother sees that man has fallen into his position and she touches her cheek to his and hands him Baby Girl and moves his hands to hold her in the correct way.

The three, as a procession, move slowly towards the water and the laughing gurgling there seems to quiet. This liquid spirit, this giver of life and reflecting place, is the first introduction and Baby Girl will know the water and the water will know Baby. At the bank, at the edge, the white gentle waters fold upon themselves and speak and murmur and sing to Baby. Her eyes open wide, and she stirs the air around her with arms and with her legs. She is seeking the touch and Father hands Baby to Mother and she kneels and places the baby's feet ankle deep in the water. In this way water and Baby do meet. Mother is washing Baby's feet and tiny toes, placing the droplets on her cheeks and washing her neck. Baby shivers and laughs and wriggles to be free, wanting more, more, more of the laughing spirit, the life-giving spirit, Water.

Now others draw near, each waiting respectfully for their turn to greet. Fish and crawfish, snake and bird, the rabbit, the wolf, coyote and bird, all draw near. It is the introducing time, and the conversation is a question and a revealing.

Here is our relation, and here. We are one puzzle, many pieces and each incomplete without the other. We give, you give, we share amongst us an understanding and an appreciation of the One-ness and on this we all agree.

Man is awed and there is only a tiny, tiny part of him that recognizes that he no longer understands the languages of the many nations; the knowing is not gone, only his attention is elsewhere. If he could but look, could but listen, it would all come flooding back, but he is deaf and blind and full of this new intention and he will only reminisce and sorrow over the loss of language when he must kill to eat or to clothe. All is now in relation to his daughter and for him it seems as if he is on one side of her and the world on the other, and only she holds them both at once.

* * *

Woman with child is a brand new being too. She feeds the baby and cooks for the Man and there is in her an ancient sort of understanding that escapes all but the oldest most awakened of men. She sees the cycle and accepts the movement and can sit and wipe sweat from a sick person's brow and sing low and lullaby and tireless and though not aloof, decidedly separate. The mother role is the earth or the moon, some of the people say the sun, either way it has its own gravitational field, its own weight, and its own wisdom.

* * *

Woman/Mother hums her songs and holds and washes her baby and watches her Man and she is pleased. Her wild urges to fly, to race storms and dance atop trees made of fragile flowers is temporarily quelled and she only gazes long into the flames as if gazing into the future.

***

Man is a hunter now. He roams far and away and sits still for long hours wondering, or not. He is away from his Woman and his child because he is unnecessary there, extra, and underfoot. So, he searches for meat while they have plenty and he roams and watches the waters flow and tree limbs sway and bounce. Sometimes he drags his feet and goes slow and each time, every time he returns to his home, he waits out of sight, out of range. He stands and looks closely, waiting for some sign.

He smells the home smoke and feels the warmth and the closeness, and the contentment and yet he circles around and around, he has become perimeter Man, circling around a center of himself that he can never know. His is a pleasant sort of confusion, and he shuffles about until he senses a small gap, lapse, energetic glitch and then slides into the groove there and is pulled, as if from outside himself, forward to hearth, to family, to a something he longs for and yet cannot hold, even when immersed and bathed in its familial feel.

And Man's vulnerability sits low in his belly, a small cold seed needing only some measure of fear to sprout, waiting patient, all the time in the world, breathing the Man like it is his center.

Peripheral Man

Weeks roll out and pass like clouds, floating first
white and fluffy, amorphous, intangible to touch,
enormous to eye then burning away in the bright
light of sun. Peripheral man, perimeter man,
unnecessary, extra, Superfluous Man wanders
farther and farther from home, ambling, strolling,
walking, just walking, hour upon hour after hour.
He is hunting though they've plenty of meat, he is
scouting though he knows the land very well. Man
is scattering himself all over the land, then trying to
collect himself and find himself and determine who,
what, how does he make sense?

Woman and Child are entwined, symbiotic and
necessary to one another. Their connection grows
and Child's glowing shapes shift and entwine and
twirl about, glowing brighter and snaking over her
body declaring power and power and Woman
Mother is guiding her and she is speaking with the
other nations and they are educating her. Awkward
Man sits outside the warmth of the fire and

watches in wonder as the two collaborate and create a world, a life where he is but an accessory.

Man swims in the lakes and douses in the stream. He climbs high in the trees and lays on the branches feeling the sway, the to and fro of the wind. He can no longer converse with the animal nations, and the grasses obey the wind not him. He does not care, nor belabor the point. He is pleased enough to walk mile after mile, day after day, turning browner and growing stronger and healthier.

And so, Man begins to feel apart.

A separateness, a certain invisibility comes and claims him, and it soothes the nagging fear in his belly, relieves him of the worry and doubts. He is finding his freedom in being extraneous and his days are like sighs, content, empty save for the beauty of the land and the sky, the water and the lives of the various peoples going about their daily business, living, eating, having sex, growing old and passing on and he watches not wholly detached because he finds some comfort in the turning of the wheel, the unspooling of one life leading directly to the first tug of a new long thread of another and another and so on and on and over and over.

And Man at last finds the peace of knowing that he does not matter.

***

At six years of age Child notices Man. She is already
wise and already strong and there is a stillness that
sits with her and washes through her and
sometimes the glowing lines will quiet and settle
and dim and in those moments the Child can be
mistaken for an elder in mien, in description. Of
course, she IS still six and there can be small storms
and cruelties and small, small fights, conflicts and
pecking order skirmishes. And Man is bewildered
and vaguely disconcerted! as he does not
understand why there is struggle, why is there this
defining of roles of barriers of hierarchy? Isn't it
clear that he stands watch at the wall? That he does
not even wish to sit at the table, only make sure
that there is plenty on it and that it is arranged just
so.

Man is merely support staff. He feels no ambition
and so the posturing and testing and rearranging
that is a small child figuring out where they are
positioned is all beyond him. He only feels that
sometimes the wind and the grasses bear him
farther from the shelter and there are occasional

curtains drawn and shimmering optical fences to dissuade his approaches and hold him away and he sighs contentment and sleeps in the grass, sleeping soft on the knowledge that his people are warm and dry and protected from the elements.

***

It is spring and the trees with barren branches have suddenly grown small green buds. There are great cracking and booming sounds and though the mornings are cold, there is a time in the middle of the day, when the sun warms the skin just so and all sane creatures stop and turn their face to the sun and closing their eyes accept the warmth and the bright white yellow light shining red through their eyelids. Everyone enjoys the softening of their bones, the new energies shining up and down and moving through and into them, and it is as if the whole world takes pause and soaks, basks in the warm light and for a moment relaxes.

Grasses are sprouting bright green and low, close to the ground, not yet taking over for the silver browns that have survived the winter snows. It is birthing season and born. Man feels the tug and pull and turns his face towards home. Lithely he rolls, up to his feet, and off the great stone, where he has been sun soaking like some smooth, brown reptile warming his blood.

Man had lain atop the rock for hours, the brightness of the sky hurting his eyes, until he draped an arm across his lids and blocked it all out. His thoughts drift to Woman and her softness and goodness, her flashing smiles and compassionate eyes, even her rare occasional annoyance, and he absent mindedly scrubs the skin on his arms where the shapes of magic no longer glow.

He remembers their nights together, the warm blankets and the times when they stayed inside long after sunrise, unwilling to dis-entangle themselves from one another. And Man feels a rushing sense of longing and melancholy and it is absorbed into this great feeling of fullness, fullness that comes when he watches his Woman and his Child weave or sew, gather or grind grasses and herbs. Man can watch them all day and never tire. It is only when Woman traces the curves and the shapes and moves in such a way as to conjure the waves and swirls that he turns away. And in those moments, next to his vulnerability, lies a small seed of resentment. He cannot bend the grasses or call the clouds anymore.

Woman sleeps

Woman sleeps. It seems she has not in at least six years.

There are nights when she falls exhausted into the blankets and lies motionless, unconscious for a few hours sure, but this cannot be called sleep. Sleep is a nurturing thing, a healing time when the sleep spirit rises up and out of the body and flies through the landscape of the mind, testing, experimenting, exploring and finding the occasional hidden truth, leaving the brow a little less furrowed and the shoulders a little less raised; this is sleep and Woman is having her first in many years.

Child watches and she does see Woman's dreams and she is filled with questioning and curiosity. There is the Man and the Woman, and Child is moved by the energies flowing back and forth between them, it is not love in any language she understands. It is not the insistent need of the animal nations when they make the new lives, it is not the warmth, the bottomless strength expressed through the Woman's arms and face when she holds the Child close and murmurs low. It is some altogether different thing this partnership of sorts.

How does Man who drifts in and out of Child's awareness hold this place in Woman's dreams? What is this collaboration of two disparate beings?

And as Child watches it slowly comes into focus that these two large humans have merged, blurred, boundaries. There is a space where Man and Woman exist that is undimmed by argument or space. Child sees that she herself is the very center of Man and Woman's relationship and so he, plain and strong and brown and vague, and She warm, deep-strong and wise are as one in purpose, in dream.

Child turns her face towards Man.

Man is an uncomplicated picture. He turns his eyes to the Woman and takes her direction in all things. Most mornings he is gone early to the forest. He leaves unremarked and returns, as a softly falling far away breeze, barely ruffling the leaves. And the grasses only move at his touch.

Child sees her Mother's softening features, watches her breath rise and fall, swirls a finger through her dreams, stirring and watching as they settle into a scene of Woman in Man's arms, face to a fire, absorbed by the flickering orange and yellow visions and warmed by the contentment generated between the two.

Turning to Man, the daughter Child moves to him and beckons him.

Follow.

He looks around in some confusion, so she calls directly to him, and gestures,

Out.

And so, they move outside, and the flap softly falls, closed.

***

Girl is looking at his face directly, unflinchingly, and while at first Man feels some small discomfit, he gazes back and holds open his face self so Girl may look. Man has no space to protect or hide, he only stands without thought, empty of fear or expectation, and Girl having completed her inspection and questioning, reaches out and holds Man's hand and pulls him. She wants him to show her his way.

She is small. Man is tall and strong and lithe. But it is clear who holds power here.

The two of them move through the fresh green grasses, quiet and soft as a gentle wind, the vibrant green blades part and vee, both in front and behind. Father and Daughter create a singular wake, the same as any vessel slicing smoothly through, still lake waters.

Man pauses and turns, motioning to Girl and shushing her with his hand. He pulls her tiny hand down and lets her palm graze across the tops of the long leaves, feeling the scratchy tingling, sensation of it. Girl looks up to Man questioning, she has never touched the grasses on purpose. Man smiles and sits down and removes his soft shoes. And bids Girl do the same and she does.

Rising to their feet, a look of wonder comes, Girl with her bare feet on the ground, her hands on the tip-top tongues of the tall springy grasses can feel the pulling, magnetic power of earth, the soft continuity of the fields of green, they are smooth like the unbroken surface of some body of water. She can feel dirt and its particular, peculiar, connecting texture and grounding and the lightness of the wavering grasses and the duality of the mountain and the sky, cloud and tree...Girl is discovering the difference between theory and practice, dreamy power and earthy immersion. She is magic and theory and Man, he is thirst, dirt and the smell of horse sweat.

She waves him forward,

More, show me more.

And so, they move farther, down to the banks of the silver stream and kneel to touch, to wait, to close eyes and listen. The tumbling laughter of the water speaks and sparkles and drawing a deep breath to smell the earthiness of the water now, to see on the surface, water children darting here and there, playing, and she is smelling the water, deeper, slower, the still places of eddy and pool and depth and a shiver goes through Girl's spine, and she opens her eyes. Man softly pulls her hand into the coolness and feeling the fire of it and the thudding cold of it and the pressing and gentle but insistent pushing, as the water moves without questioning, it goes where it must go, this is nature.

Girl is wide eye-ed open, watching into the man with a new awareness, new realizations, new astonishment. Mother in her focus, in her intention to train, to educate, to liberate and build the swirling universal energies into powers and flight, has neglected a piece, a part, a truth of every child. Girl is human and possessed of a body and taste and touch and sight for the real magic, the dirty, majestic earth magic of plant and bird and sky and wind.

And Man guides her cold, wet, hand from the water and into the muddy mossy, half in, half out, of the bank just there. He places the shiny bright blue and red crawfish into her tiny palm, and she is feeling the tiny stepping grasping walking feet and the brush of the powerful tail which can propel crawfish backwards at tremendous speed. She is filled with a fascination and wonder at this separate being, this crawfish is embarked on its own journey, its own life course and exploration. He is driven by needs and evolutionary demands particular only to him, and girl connected is inundated, washed over into confusion by the distinction of truths and perspective.

The crawfish reaches out its bumpy claw and grabs the soft skin on Girl's palm, the place between thumb and forefinger and pinches down hard!

Girl shrieks out in pain and her whole body jumps of its own accord and she flips the crawfish into the water and turns with tears streaming down her face to Man. It is HURT she has felt, and it is terrible and sharp and there is a beginning stab and then a residual decaying memory of pain and Man is watching and holding her tiny hand and rubbing the pain and chill away and Girl is torn between crying and wonder.

Pain, hurt, is a new thing. Where does it go? How to rearrange the magic and the rising white light with this visceral sensation of OW! And Girl is watching Man and their relationship has shifted in these moments and Man is Dad and now Girl sees, when Dad looks at her, the Love there, the deep chasm in him that is vulnerability and pride and loneliness.

Girl's head turns side to side and her eyes are staring into herself and there is a new rising understanding. From some old place, from some old magic that is more solid than lines moving and dancing on her skin comes this welling up and it is this Dad and Daughter relationship that is a falling, and a tumbling, and shows a playful sort of surface. It is dancing and reflecting light in a sparkly way and there, underneath is that depth, that still strength that will not be stopped and it is as a river.

What is this dancing energy going back and forth and rather than taking, filling? Is there anything else, any other?

And Girl places her tiny hand back inside her father's and he is dissolved, and she is lifted up and they move up to standing and walking and this time, the grasses do not part, because the touching of them, the changing scratchy soft fluttering feel of them, is more magical than any ability to move them aside.

Father and Daughter walk for these hours and these days and drink from the cold mountain streams and sit in the warming of the morning sun and eat berries so fat that they fairly burst before you can even get them to your mouth, and there are blue stains on their chins and blue stains on their fingers and laughter on their faces. Side by side they steep in the stillness that comes with the evening sun settling below the horizon. They watch it down, orange, red, pink and purple until all is still. Girl sees that all the nations pause in their busy-ness, to witness, to drink in, to absorb, to PARTICIPATE in this stillness and glory and life.

Such a strange idea that participation comes from this witnessing, this silent and still revering of creation rather than the running scurrying hurrying need to eat and drink and survive. It is not the nutrients that create participation, it is the taste. It is not the worry and plan, but recognition of this and this and now and now. Touch, taste, see and in a moment, there is all of creation and all of why we breathe.

Woman fights

The interior of the shelter is warm, dry, and smells of wood smoke, delicious stew, and all manner of medicinal herbs, examples of which hang from the shelter poles. The smoothed, worn, skins, with the flagrant splash of holy paintings, capture and contain the sounds and the smells of love making and family and life. Family...even in her sleep, even immersed in her sweetest dreams the whole large full and round path of family sparks a smile and presses a curve into her full, happy lips. All these comforts and questions and fears that she never dreamt of, expected or even knew enough to hope for, will be her path and turn her and fill her out and fill her up, with health and strength and wisdom and purpose.

Woman belongs.

She dreams of family and it is a simple sort of wonderful to be a part of something so intimate, so fragile, so temporary.

To be needed.

She is mother and lover and around her all others revolve, turn, track and trail.

And in her dream, she turns and takes off and up and into the sky and soars out to follow the tracks made by her husband and their beloved daughter. Woman spends hours here amongst the clouds, soaring high above, turning lazy spirals on the heat rising up from the soft brown and green earth below. And in these hours, there is a satisfaction, a contentment that softens and fills her heart and sometimes she dives to gain speed and spins and banks hard and twirls a dance in the air just because.

Medicine Woman loves in that way that mothers love, holding the child's happiness more dear than her own, unselfish, sacred. She watches, with a deep sense of rightness, the growing bond between her daughter and her husband. She smiles as she wonders who needs who the most. As he spends days with his daughter, Man has at last found a place where his vulnerability, his heart, feels safe. For the very first time in ever, her man knows trust.

Woman knows that as deeply and completely as he loves his wife, there is and will always be the slight reserve, the last high wall constructed of shame and embarrassment and insecurity. They do not speak of his past, but she knows, she has seen his memories. She has smelled his fear and his pain, felt as he did, the clogging drowning heavy weight of a rage so thorough that it wipes away all but the urge to murder. And more. She has tasted the cruelty that lies dormant, hibernating, waiting for the moment of betrayal, ready to leap forth and wreak horror.

In the depths of night, she has held her man close, holding him tight to quiet his shaking, shuddering, earth quaking body as his love fought its way to the surface, reaching his skin as some electric energy that is as shy as any small star on any cloudy night. And in those moments, she herself has let go and fallen, into the sweet obliteration, the ecstasy and the gone-ness. She has felt her breast push towards the heavens, reaching and straining for more touch, more depth, more of the thrilling energetic power flowing from his hands and his heart and into her and filling her with some ecstatic full love feeling that leaves her suspended in air like those frothy drops of saltwater spray splashing and crashing, an infinite part of some vast ocean crystal clear and deep and dark. She has lain with him while silent tears sprung up and filled his eyes to brimming. And she has felt the fierce power in his strong brown limbs as he moved from protector and provider to lover to animal, to desire and need.

Subtle as the fading light, easy as the symbols of magic slowly disappearing from skin, Man and Woman have grown close, intimate in the way of shared lives and loves, troubles and triumphs. The edges softened, the center shines and it is that they are in love with each other and with their child and with this life.

Medicine Woman sleeps and outside her shelter a small band of unempathetic men move silently through the wood.

These men are not bad man nor good men, they are only as they are, practical creatures, incapable of remorse or regret. For these men life is a simple and straightforward affair. Meat must be hunted and butchered and taken back to their families. There is no moral imperative beyond tribe, there is no larger conversation.

They pause just inside the shadow. They squat and look out into the clearing, peering through the trees, waiting and watching. Woman does not notice; she is dreaming and flying. Miles away, Man does not notice; he is immersed in the story of himself and daughter and falling into connection with the moment and the nature.

The small band of men rise from the ground as mist, floating to their feet and spreading out and moving on line and converging. Their feet whisper through the grasses. Their strong brown bodies swim through the thick air. Their weapons sit ready in the hand.

The animals go quiet, the breezes cease and inside the shelter Woman stirs in her dream, turning in the sky and staring back towards their home.

The knife punctures the thick hide and rips down, slicing through all the between, all the illusion of a sheltered place. And Woman is slammed into her body and comes hard awake in biting confusion and fear. The men are thrusting themselves through the walls and into the shelter. In moments, the smell of sweat and spilled food and sacked dreams and blood fills the no longer safe place, crowding out all else.

Woman is swirling to her feet and casting her blanket like a whip, uncoiling and cracking and cutting. The men are swarming over her and clogging and cloying and suffocating her and she cannot move, and she does not scream. Held as a small space, as a memory, she sees her lover's face and her daughter. She is filled with a power and shattered with it and men are flung hard back into the walls and there are cracking noises and huffs of air being crushed from lungs and the constant hissing sound of blades passing through flesh and life leaving and splashing to the ground and onto the walls and already turning from bright red to a darker deeper sadder color.

Woman fights as a fury unleashed. She is unfettered power spun up into a personal tornado of violence and precision, and the men are being beaten back, driven back, pressed away by sheer force of will. And even in their wild, hard faces there is some glint of surprise. This small band of men has taken down buffalo and cougar and warriors of many nations. They fight as an accomplished team and still the outcome is in doubt.

There is a worn and polished, hardwood handle, thick as your wrist. It is dark, stained with years of sweat and precious, used to be necessary, blood. On the end there is a stone, grey and hard and unfeeling. And the man swings it down and it connects in a final way and all Woman is and all she was, crumples to the ground looking for all the world like a dropped cloth, collapsing into and upon itself and piling up there. And the thick deep red flows through her shiny black hair and streams its way down to the earth.

The men where they have fallen to their backs or been driven to their knees sit stunned. The ferocity, the uncompromised violence of the fight has rocked them. Two of their band lay dead, heads nearly ripped from torso. None of the men are unscathed.

The man with the killing stick grunts and there is a hint of relief that comes into the air of the shelter, and then a rising anger. He stabs the stick down through the strip of rope around his waist and lets the weapon hang there, fast thickening drops of blood fall and land on his foot and streak down his leg.

He bends over grimacing and roughly takes hold of Woman's ankles and jerks her into movement, dragging her dying body along the ground, twisting and cursing angrily as he stumbles, pulling her over the fallen and the dead.

Through the doorway opening and out into the daylight, he throws her feet to the side and drops heavily and completely, full on her chest, leading with his knees. He hears the cracking bones and the unconscious moan. Growling, yelling his victory song, he draws his knife and lays it on her cheek, hoping the coolness will draw her back to this now so she can lift him up with her suffering. He believes that the gods will hear her cries of pain as signals of his greatness.

Woman is taking too long to die. She is half here and half there and struggling with the pain and the vision of her family and the brutality is happening and she is witnessing as though from a distance the desecration and the mutilation and she is without weight or substance and turns to face her family, her sweet everything and she is pulled back and away, sliding, and their features are growing faint and receding and fogging and disappearing and now, without their faces to hold her here, she can no longer bear the pain of this body. Turning in the way she has known; she leaves this now and moves into the next.

Death

Father and Daughter are resting. They sit side by side on a warm grey rock, dangling their toes in the icy water that is moving down from the high places, snow melt clear and cold as God's eye, washing sand and pebble, nuggets of gold and pieces of sky, down into the valley where they sit in quiet communion. All around them, golden grasses wave and ripple and gigantic, brown, golden elk graze with eyes that watch everywhere and low murmuring breathing sounds that relax even the shaking aspen leaves.

A slight, quick wind cuts across the valley and Girl starts and screams. The ever changing, dancing, blue and black, sometimes silver shapes on her skin have frozen for a moment and burn, they burn like day old coals, embers as they fade, flashing first brilliant orange and then cooling, covered in grey ash and dirt. The pain is excruciating, and she can only shriek over and over and cry unto the sky and the depths of hell. Loss is gripping her and swelling in her and her chest is bursting and bleeding and her heart is being torn out and still beating tossed to the ground. It is a sleepy, drowsy leaving of consciousness and mercifully she falls. Man afraid, deeply afraid, scared marrow deep in his cracking bones, catches Girl and won't let her fall hard. He sees the momentary stillness of the shapes and a desperate, hurt, groan is crushed from his chest and moves up through his throat, entering the world as a broken sob.

Father gathers Daughter tight in his arms and sprints hard across the flat valley bottom, whistling to the elk from some long-forgotten place inside himself and they, hearing, agree for reasons larger than comprehension. Man leaps astride the largest volunteer and cradling Girl in his arms, holding tight to the strong, brown, curly fur, allows himself one hitching sob. Elk turns smoothly, careful not to throw the two and building, adds speed until he is fairly flying over the ground.

Blurred moments of thundering hooves, lungs working like bellows and a small girl child burrowing deeper into the Man's chest and arms and security and seeking respite, shelter, refuge from the dead feeling that is being born in her chest. Man is numb but for an icy sprout of fear. The valley is going grey and chill, drops of mist gather and the animal nations scurry to shelter and hush their small families. Elk slows to a walk and then stands, chest heaving, to replace the oxygen burned, trying hard to find purchase in this new slippery reality.

There is a rolling roiling feel and dark clouds tumble over themselves, rolling like boulders, cracking and thudding and vibrating the very heart of every living being.

And Man spies the blood stained grass and falls to his knees, Girl child spilling out of his arms and collapsing into the ground.

It is an earthquake, a cataclysm and the parts of him, the pieces of him are shifting and drifting about and finding no purchase he is becoming unmoored and unhinged and a madness fogs his eyes and he cannot see anything other than the trail, the prints, the indications. He follows to where Woman lays ruined and soaked in what was her life, her hair still shiny but the rest... the rest an empty thing, a corpse, a place devoid of animation or life,

Man has only a silent, screaming, wailing black hole where his soul had been a moment before. He is on the ground and all he can see are blades of grey grass and all he can smell is dirt and blood and there is a rising dark hatred coiling up, filling him up. Like waking snakes, the poisonous lines of power are burning back onto his skin and the symbols are coiling and hissing with pain. They describe shapes of power and portend death. Lost in his hatred and grief Man does not notice that Girl child is being pulled apart and the lines are lifting off her skin and there are scars, and she writhes in agony. He does not notice at all and she cannot speak, and her movements are smaller and smaller and shrinking into her clothing, finally becoming only twitches and flutters. In these moments, her life is as fragile as the wings of a small butterfly, as thin as the tendril of smoke rising into the sky from a fire already quenched and out, only singing its song of leaving.

And Man, he sees only black, bitter, gone-ness and the decay that has already begun. And the animals flee his presence, and he is lifted to his feet and pulled into the sky by the pain that pierces his skin like sharp carved bone tied to some demon bird's claws. A demon bird that is winging up into a storm from whence he will not return.

Girl lies motionless and still. The tension is all gone from her, and her hair falls from her face and pours into the surrounding blades of grass and her eyes drift like clouds seeing nothing but sky and mist. All she has left are small shudders and a trembling.

Four days gone and no food, no water. Girl sits and rocks herself slowly, back and forth, her hair hangs in her face and her face is grief and gray and empty of all but sorrow. She moans low and hurt and it is enough that the grasses droop and the branches droop and nothing will ever be straight again.

Man sits and rocks as well, to and fro, back and forth, and it is a madness building in him, taking over his every thought, cell, follicle and grain. His eyes are feverish and dark sparking and show nothing but a callous contempt. He cannot look at the Girl only past her, near her, under and over and sometimes glancing across the surface of her but never connecting, never looking at her, connecting with her. She is a blank place in his mind, where he dares not go. The risk is too much, too high, the split, the divide, would sunder him in two and so he does not acknowledge her presence at all as anything other than a rock, a fallen tree, a corpse, something to step over or around on his way to oblivion.

Man has markings again. He is the Bad Man... again. The shapes are back, and they fairly hiss across his skin, malevolent and sick. The smell of burning flesh is on him, and he is a sort of black hatred which causes the animals to avoid his presence, they make wide circles around him and do not wander near.

Bad Man's obsidian eyes move across the bent grasses, the dry, brown, blood stain and the remains of his wife, his love, his redeeming heart. He sees the glowing prints and the story of violence written there. Woman asleep, resting deeply and only waking when it was far too late as the first hammer blows struck her and hurt her and broke her. He sees that her last thoughts were of her Man, her love, and her Girl, her very reason. Bad Man watches and sighs, when the curtain of unconsciousness dropped and relieved Woman of her pain.

And she did die there, leaking her life into the dirt, her spirit going gone and there was no song from her.

The savage end of her life and those who took it were as plain to the bad man as any morning sunrise. And it is true that the Great Mother shared deeply enough in his anguish, in his sense of loss, that she did not intervene in his growing hate, but allowed. There is a balance in some way, even if way beyond any human understanding.

Bad Man rises to his feet and turns east to follow.

Vengeance

Vengeance, retribution, these words do not describe the Bad Man's thoughts. His mind spares no space for defining. He is death, black as an abyss. Having once known light, he is now the more impenetrable for it, a place with no light from stars or moon, no wisp of any good thing remaining. He is become a singularity, and he moves to hunt, to kill, to murder, to erase from this earth any and all who had any connection to the death of his beloved.

***

Little Girl frail, on the fourth day has been visited by the spirits and is knowing her way. This morning ghosts came to her and they touched softly the scars left behind, the marks of powers gone from her. On her skin there remain only pale reminders etched a lighter color than her brown-red, sun burned skin. The ghosts, they did not comfort her. They did straighten her and fill her with breath and pulled her to her feet and told her to LIVE. Follow the Bad Man and live. And Girl Frail turned her eyes upon her father and saw that he was gone and in his place was death and she understood that she was to follow death and be its rebuke.

Girl Frail is pulled straighter, and her eyes do show a dim fire, a small spark of purpose and she turns and begins to walk. One step after another.

And she follows the Bad Man, the Hurt Man.

***

Rabbit flees and in his thunder thumping heart he does not see or think and smashing into the trunk of a small sapling, he ceases to be and lies motionless, unconsciousness. Girl Frail picks him up and whispers a prayer of sorrow and of thanks and dispatches rabbit quickly and as mercifully as she can. Building the fire in the way of her father, she cooks rabbit and eats. There is a warmth, and it moves from her tummy out to the end reaches of her limbs and she will live, and she will follow and witness and wait. One day her father will return, and she will grieve her mother.

Bad Man moves forward along the trail of the ones who murdered his love. He drifts just above the ground like a tendril of fog chasing back out to the sea. He floats, and he eats rage, and the burning inside him is enough and when he occasionally stoops to drink from some stream, he does not see himself, his reflection there. He sees time streaming by and changing the grasses and the dead twigs, and the crawfish flee from his presence and Bad Man is as relentless, as the water. His traveling feels as a stream, a river moving down slope, inexorable. His breath and his footfalls are silent, and leaves fall dead and brown all around him.

***

Bad Man smells the smoke and the cooking food. He hears the murmur of conversation and jest, the rubbing sound of buckskin on stone and rawhide on wood. His feet do not slow but they do not hurry. They press forward as water does, flowing and fitting to the circumstance, but never wavering, offering no relief, relentless. He is moving towards the things that hurt his Love, the things that birthed him.

The grass is brown and wilted, the air is heavy and dull and sound does not travel. Bad Man does not curve or deviate from his straight line forward. He strolls towards the first man-thing the same as he strolls to the horizon, to a meal, to a tree, towards nothing at all. The man-thing there sees a creature, a specter walking towards him. Bad Man is mesmerizing in his consistency. His total lack of emotion leaves him nothing but a sort of void in space and he never really looks at the man, just past him, near the edges of him, seeing a shape more than a man.

Bad Man smells of death and dirt and blood and at the very last moment the man-thing feels the hair on his arm stand straight up and a chill race through his nervous system. It is all he feels as he is lifted off his feet and into the air and there is an audible crack. He is shaken once, loose, limp and dead and then his body is dropped unceremoniously to the ground. He is as dead and done as the gutted and drained carcass of a deer that hangs from a nearby tree branch. His body lays loose and steaming like a pile of entrails.

The second and third man-things hear the crack and turn and watch their companion die. So out of any context they recognize as violence is the experience, that at first, they are stunned and curious rather than afraid. They do not move, only stupidly stand, trying to work out what is happening.

Bad Man at last raises his eyes enough to take in the small clearing. He sees the two men frozen for a moment and some movement begins just above his ears and rolls over his head and down through his neck running outwards over his shoulders and down to his fingers. His back relaxes in a wave and even his feet seem to soften their connection with the ground.

The shapes on his skin are coiling and spitting and hissing and burning. His skin roiling like storm clouds, he turns to stare at the farther man. There the meat softens and falls from the bones and the man is trying to scream. He is becoming a sort of sack or bag of meat and cannot stand without bones. And so, he melts, down into the dirt, only a long low keening wail of pain escapes him in continuous song. And Bad Man turns.

The last man thing is no coward. He is hardened and tough from a lifetime of skirmishes and combat, trickery and cruelty and death. He is intimately acquainted with death; and so, he sees who is here and he immediately begins to sing his death song. The cry is strong in his voice and unafraid and slightly fierce even.

It really does not matter at all. He dies as quickly and as easily as the first two.

The Bad Man ghosts to the fire and sits, where moments before the now dead thing had sat. He raises a bowl to his lips and drinks the bone broth and the fat and the taste and the soup runs down his chin and drips into the earth and mingles there with the blood of the last man ended. He does not feel relief. There is no elation. There is no feeling at all. He is hungry for the first time in a week and so he eats. The food, a traveler's stew rich in every nutrient needed to move, to be warm, to cross vast expanse and murder and rape does not fill the empty place inside him. Bad Man's skin still crawls and undulates and the shapes of power coil and set themselves and Bad Man is still death.

***

Girl Frail is hungry.

It has been days since she cooked and ate, days following in the wake of her father, no longer her father. Forgotten are the days spent wandering through the forest hand in hand, sitting and watching for hours as the birds and the animals slowly acclimate to their presence and fetch up close. The moving diagrams are mostly gone from her skin, only light-colored scars remain, reminders of the shapes of joy and fascination, enchantment, and serenity. They mark her, but they do not move, there is no power there. All her powers now come from the gifts of awareness and connection; the days spent with her father becoming a citizen of this visceral world.

***

All the becoming's acquainted with heat and cold, the shivering thrill of snow melt water dancing across her tiny toes, these are her strengths now. The feeling of knowing hunger low in her belly and thirst and the sense of reverence and awe when you see this world of dirt and flesh, these are her treasures. Pain and mountain, sky, and the tiny hairs on the backs of her arms, watching as vultures circle round and round with no flap of their wings, soaring ever higher on the invisible spiraling waves that distort the vision and carry the air high to the heavens, these moments are the magic she owns now.

Yes. She can build and use fire. She can find water and construct shelter. She can pray and sing and dance and call on those supporting energies, but she cannot bend the grass or bring the clouds, those things happen of their own accord, those things happen, and they possess their own magic. Girl Frail's power is that she can acknowledge, she can witness, she can revere, and she can fall into a gratitude so profound that the animal nations willingly sacrifice themselves and die so as to join her, to become a part of her gratitude song.

This is the magic that carries her forward, step upon step. Girl moves forward as relentless as the Bad Man, only, sometimes she pauses. Her eyes move over the devastation left by him and the ugliness of neglect, and she does direct her attention and maybe, just maybe a small blade of grass lifts a bit, raises itself towards that which sees and too, maybe it is just the breeze gently shooing away the stench of Death.

Girl Frail is hungry; and so, she sits on the stump of tree next to the fire and she spoons stew into the bowl. She drinks and chews and with each mouthful she feels the energy soaking in. Even before she swallows, her mouth is absorbing the nutrients, the warmth is returning to her bones and her tissues are filling up and filling out and as she moves back into her body the pain there begins to move. Girl Frail sits and eats, and tears stream down her cheeks.

To live is to hurt.

Some deep knowing, some deep remembering, allows her to understand that this new pain, this feeling of bereavement and loss and separation and grief is somehow no different than the feeling of cold or hunger or sun burned skin. It does hurt, it must hurt. This pain too is part of the magic, and human existence must be this way.

The dead men's stew does taste good.

Girl Frail is slow to swallow. The warmth on her face from the fire and its light push back the dark and the cold left by the Bad Man. The same flame that warms her can burn and will kill as fast, as dispassionately, as the cold and the dark. Girl Frail absorbs these thoughts and feelings and knowings and begins to build some structure, some skeleton to hang these wisdoms upon.

As Girl fills up, she raises her eyes and sees about her. She notes the tamped down blades of grass laying helter-skelter, pointing here and there, the tie line laying loose on the ground, the horses milling about there, aimless. She sees the braided lariat leads and she sees the fresh cuts into small branches. She sees the drag trail of dead wood brought to build a fire. She sees the dead men. They lay twisted and broken and surprised that their time was over so quickly.

Girl stands, turning her head in the direction her Not Father has taken. He is already out of sight, moving restlessly, relentlessly, just as the seasons. Bad Man is on the trail, on the hunt, following his nature. He will kill them all, every last one.

And Girl is pulled heart first, dragged as the dead wood was dragged to the fire, to the body of the first man killed. He lays broken, head nearly torn from his body, in a grotesque shape no living human could create. And Small Girl falls softly to her knees there. The grasses, the earth, the mother receives her gently and supports her there. Girl is no stranger to dead things, and she is not repulsed nor uncomfortable. Filled only with a strange curiosity, a child's sense of wonder, she reaches out and touches the dead man's finger pads. They are hard and calloused and not yet cold. She turns his hand and looks at his palm. She takes note of the lines there and the scars and all the evidences that the dead man had once been unique.

She pulls his arm and arranges his body a bit and studies the stitches in his leggings, the dyed quills in their hopeful shapes added to his shirt by someone. Or maybe he had stolen it from another dead man who had taken it from another. The feelings in the small Girl go swirling through her and she takes careful hold of the dead man's shirt and tries to move him and cannot. And so, she stands and fetches water from the bladders hung at the nearest shelter's entry. She returns and kneels by the dead man and does wash his face. Hesitant at first, she tenderly brushes the hair out of his face. This was the man who murdered her Mother. And in a twitch, in a disembodied fury, she pulls his knife from the sheath on his hip and plunges the blade into his chest over and over. There is no blood, his heart has long ago stopped, but she stabs him again and again anyway and does sing her mother's name.

Footsteps

Footsteps, footfalls, one after one and another, these days all seem to follow some strange terminal rhythm. Bad Man moves like time. Without deviation or consideration for thirst, hunger, sleep, cold or hot, uphill, down, he has no thought save the constant drumming need to kill, to eradicate without joy, without regret, every single being attached to those who have killed his love.

Girl trails slow, drifting behind. She is quiet but quickening. Her eyes have at last begun to flick around with some interest, and she notes the shifting of the wind and the shapes of floating, passing, clouds. The sweet fragrance of pine needle does occasionally crack through the odor of death that follows her Not Father and she feels the effects course through her body.

How strange that a scent can speed, spin, or calm the heart, quicken the blood and stir pangs of hunger. A remembered smell can cause tears to sprout forth, from eyes that were dry only moments before. These things she notices. Girl's feet have become strong yet sensitive. She has discarded footwear and goes barefoot forwards, crossing fields of stone, cold swift streams and warm dark lichens, and grasses, and raw dirt earth, and she is cleaner there, on the soles of her feet than she is on her neck behind and underneath her lengthening dark hair.

And she does finally see, that her hands are blood stained on their backs, while her palms are clean and fresh. And she does note that perhaps it is better to walk and to work, than hide in the dark recesses near the back of her brain. And so, each day she washes her hands on the grass, she carefully arranges her sleeping spaces, and she stops collecting bowls and spoons and combs and begins to create these things for herself.

Girl begins to allow memories of her Mother Love to come, and with it an ache that is overwhelming. She allows a pain, that like dark high clouds, blots out the light, and chills her to her very core.

Mother, mommy, mama, love.

With her mother there had been created a special, specific, density, some shared awareness thickened the air, as sticky sweet and viscous as honey. Girl had never smelled a world without her mother's smell in it before these death filled days. Now, it is all she knows.

And so, when walking innocent, tuned to the sound of the song of the bird and the light reflecting off the trees' scratchy skins, she catches a hint, a taste, a remembrance of Mom, Mother, Mommy and tears, she is driven to her knees and prone to her face.

Girl licks her lips and knows the taste of salty tears, tears that fall until she is too fatigued to cry anymore and there is only the dirt, the dirt and the earth giving off its fertile, sun baked smells. And Girl hears the low long wail of grief that is squeezed out of her, crushed out of her like her very last breath by the weight of the remembering. And she is laying there and surrendering, falling into that place where death is close. She is reaching out her hands and her arms and striving, reaching, stretching, straining to grasp, to hold on to the end, end, end and sweet oblivion.

Girl falls into the black abyss and down.

Until she is falling up, through the green blue water with the mercury surface and bursting up and out and into the lower place.

Here there is green and green and mountains rising high into a brilliant blue sky, with crowns of white cloud or snow. And there is the low muted murmur of every living thing noting her sudden appearance from down beneath below, the clouded unknown depths.

Girl is gasping and sputtering and swimming to shore. It is covered by a curious white sand and guarded by dark sentinel boulders, craggy with age and wear. She moves through the water and her thin brown legs slice through the thickness and carry her swift up onto the warmth of the sand. The birds give her a nod of acknowledgement and welcome her back to this place she has been before, has been forever.

Mother, Mother, Mom

Girl cries out but there is no sound. She cannot speak here. She cannot eat here, only breathe and listen and witness and fly, moving amongst the trees and the rocks and the everything that is. Girl has been a gentle breeze laughing. She is not laughing this time, she is weeping softly and though there is no sound, the silver shine of tears tracking down her brown cheeks calls out and draws the animal nations forth. And they do come to wonder.

Turning to her left towards some gravity, some density, some heaviness, she sees the Old Man Buffalo. He is dark like the almost black leaves that lay at the bottom of still waters. His face is as lined and craggy as the rocks on the beach. His eyes are still and clear. His gnarled hands could be the surfaced roots of some ancient tree, brown and swollen here into knobs, there into strained thin and searching bones, grasping at the soil for life. The skin of the buffalo hangs heavy on him and it is good because otherwise he might float away. The old skin is holding him to the ground, to the earth and giving him a place amongst the lost.

Old Man Buffalo has eased close to Girl. He shows her his palms, and they are soft, and pale as papyrus and lined and old as the buffalo nation, and kind. His hands are kind and gentle and they move in swirling patterns and shapes and stir the energies in the air, collecting and shaping, giving color too it all, he pushes the truth forward towards Girl.

Truth moves onto her and around her and through her and she is inhaling deep, and the knowing is going through her and filling her with light and erupting here and there in faint glowing shapes of Love and Compassion and some understanding.

Girl, eyes closed, sees the origins of suffering, the fullness of grief and the necessity of it. She sees how the assimilation of suffering is turning her into who she must be. As gently as is possible she is changing in a kind and beautiful way.

And she is larger.

Animal people have paused in their comings and goings. They watch Girl change with connection, feeling their own swelling understanding and acceptance and gratitude as all are moved to be larger, kinder, more still, more quietly, deeply, profoundly present. And Girl Beautiful opens her eyes to thank the Old Man Buffalo and he is only a large beast standing and shifting his enormous body from side to side, each huffing breath, each gusting exhale is old and steady and stable. The buffalo breathing is as a mountain, always there, always was, always everlasting.

The most tender smile grows on Girl Beautiful's face. She is still softly crying but they are different tears now, changed.

Soft as a sigh, Girl Beautiful slips back into the water warm, and stroking away from the sand and the valley and the great lowing beast, she takes a deep breath and folds over into a dive. Slicing down into the depths, the darkness returns and then she is laying there once again, on the forest floor.

The sun has moved in the sky.

***

Girl Beautiful awakens and starts to rise and she cannot. She is lashed round her wrists and her ankles. The vines that twine around her limbs are wrapped tight around the small trunks of sapling trees. Just beginning their lives, certain as teenagers, the adolescent trees ignore the questions Girl Beautiful asks.

She lays her head back to rest on the soft brown needles and stares up through the evergreen needles and the swaying limbs of the older trees and exhales long and full. She feels the skin of salt left on her cheeks, and the cracking of it as a rueful smile comes slow to her face.

***

Later, there is still the faint scent of her mother, floating just out of reach, tantalizing, and calling. But Girl can live with her grief now, live with the scent of memories, as she understands more of the many layers of life.

There is no,

this one is real and this one is dream.

Only,

Here we must eat.

And there,

We are in prayer.

She is not caught between two worlds, or three or more, she is all at once. As she finds her acceptance, the small, nearly hidden, shapes of light spiral off of her skin and begin to unwrap the tendrils, the vines that hold her, and free Girl Beautiful, one limb and another. And she places her hands behind her head as a pillow and closes her eyes breathing deeply and feeling the world around her breathe.

Girl Becomes

She does not see the kill. And, after so many villages, so many camps and gathering spots, she should not be shocked by the blood-soaked grass, the stench of entrails and burning flesh. She has seen it all before, here vomit, there limbs, torn from their bodies. The heavy, weighted, smothering, blanket feel of death hanging over an entire area same as fog sitting over water that is warmer than the air above, is familiar to her.

But there, over there, lies the broken body of a Girl Formerly Beautiful just like her. She seems so small and wrong, lifeless.

When the breeze lifts an errant strand of hair that is not crusted thick with dried blood, the sight is so delicate and so evocative of the dead girl as a whole, and so contagious, so near the small fragile feeling that Girl Beautiful carries in her chest, in her belly, in her hands and face and eyes, that she is stunned into stillness.

Standing there as the familiar scenes and sights of yet another of her Not Father's bloodbaths fade;

Standing there as the stark now-ness of the small child murdered and ended, not in some eruption of rage but in the nonchalant, practiced, almost indifferent way of her Not Father's murders, grows...

Girl is overcome.

Perhaps for the first time she does not see herself as apart from the hell her Not Father delivers. She is not a witness anymore but a participant. What had existed as a vague pulling becomes a stark choice.

Girl Beautiful is no killer. She is not Death's song embodied.

Then what am I?

Again, the slight strand of the dead girl's hair lifts and floats for a moment on the breath of the gentle breeze. Girl Beautiful knows what the Buffalo Man has shown her. She feels a tender sadness steal into her heart. This is the dying of her childhood.

There is the little girl, dead, murdered.

And there is Girl herself.

And as Girl's small child-self leaves her Now teen body and goes to lie next to the small girl dead, there is the pressing in, the rushing in, of being filled with some sweet sadness.

There is born in her heart, some small, discrete grief, which Girl knows she will bear with her wherever she goes and forever more.

Girl finds herself kneeling next to the small child and reaching and smoothing and straightening and tucking. She gathers small flowers and places them soft side down on the small child's eyes. She stands and goes to the woods and gathers the fragrant grasses and the small pieces of this place so that the little girl gone will not feel like a stranger where she is.

The knowing she has is not hers, it is as old as the very first people, who when lost, found ritual and ceremony to mark their places. And Girl collects the small seedlings and the small stones, and she prays over the fire in the way that she has been shown, the ways that she has been taught. For the first time in forever she does not wonder about the direction of her Not Father. She is here now. And she takes due time and due care with the construction of the platform. She ties the knots with care and total attention, each one a separate prayer, a separate song. When Girl is finished, she moves to the small body and lifts, carries her and places her carefully in her bed of the soft and the fragrant and the beautiful. There, she is surrounded by the necessities and by small reminders of this time, this place.

Girl sits down, feels the warmth of earth under her and carefully takes drum in hand and begins the rhythmic soft notes. Rocking and closing her eyes and singing from the center of her, she feels the little girl gone and falls to her.

They cannot speak here; touch is not the same and carries no comfort.

Little Girl Gone is confused. She stands forlorn, looking round her in waiting. Girl approaches and hands her the pinecone, the cracked open and dry half shell of a small, blue, bird's egg and a salvia. The small child's eyes brighten, and her mouth opens but no words issue forth. There is only a sighing sound of peace and recognition and comfort. Little Girl Gone folds her hands and facing full on to Girl, she raises her chin and opens her eyes and opens her face and opens her heart. Her hands move close to her chest and clasp there for a moment, before they reach out towards Girl in the way of gifting, over and over until four times. It is her thanks and her heart she has given Girl. Girl is feeling the fuller fullness. There is a small pressure behind her eyes and there is the leaking, and where Girl's tears fall there are immediately the small tear flowers of this place and not of the other. They explode into blossom and lift the small girl child up and up.

The crying flowers lift Girl up higher, too.

The two fly up and above the ground. And Girl smiles and it is wan and full of some melancholy thing that resembles sorrow and gratitude and love all in one. And the Girl is back to the here and the drum's song is speeding and louder and done.

Girl sits in silence and searches around with her eyes and then standing, places the drum carefully next to the small child's body. She inhales deep and feels the new person inside her. And being wise, she does not rush but allows the feeling to travel through her body to the tips of her fingers and her toes and to rise-up, to her crown.

Girl feels a sort of peace she has never known. She has the understanding that her own brokenness has been necessary to make more room and now she is larger and in this new expansion there is room for peace and a deep knowing serenity. Girl is knowing that with each growth there must be a cracking, a breaking and a reassembly.

Girl strides over to the still glowing embers and stokes the fire back into a vivid existence. Finding the pitch and the grass, she creates a torch and singing loudly, as loudly as she can, she walks the whole of the camp and lights it afire and it does go up in high flames and thick grey smoke.

In the smoke are the prayers she has sang out with all of her being and the prayers are rising up and up to the heavens and the eagle swings round and round. And the Bad Man turns and looks up at the sky for the very first time since his love did die. He sees the smoke there and some clicking thing happens and falls into place and acceptance and he sighs and resumes his merciless hunt.

He will kill them all, each and every one.

Medicine Girl

Rhythms

Like a gentle melody, the days come together; odd notes here and odd notes there, they come together and begin to make sense. A new life-song begins to play out and be heard and danced to and hummed by Girl. She walks after Bad Man. He is easy to follow. His is the baseline, the low notes reverberating out into this place and this time. Following him is as easy as feeling the vibrations in her chest where it rests against the heart. Time and time again and far too many, and far too much, Girl enters the devastation, the wreckage left by her Not Father. She touches the dead and cleans the space and sings the death songs for those who cannot sing for themselves. And the dead touch her, each and all leave their individual marks on her. She weeps with the pain and the sorrow the Bad Man trails in his wake. His trail is stark and wide, far larger than footprints in mud or broken branches. The Bad Man leaves a trail marked and littered with broken hearts, broken bodies and broken people. He is easy to follow.

Is it three camps later or thirty? There is no counting in this way, the tragedy is too large to number. One morning just after sunup, Girl carefully moves into the latest devastation. She is accustomed to the scene, she is surrounded by the broken and the forever gone but there, just there lays a young woman who still breathes. This cannot be accidental.

The implications, the revelation that Bad Man may have some remaining piece of humanity, some small spark of Father left inside him freezes the Girl in her tracks. It seems he has left this smashed and broken person for her to put back together, to reclaim. This new information, this new possibility cannot find a place to land in Girl's mind. There are the bodies and there is the young woman and Girl is aware of the sharp pang of fear in her heart. She does not know how to bring this young woman back to the present, to this life, to this body. It is a desperate and helpless feeling.

Desperation comes and Girl feels the spiraling, coiling, singeing movements on her skin. She is calling and calling and begins to run. She runs up and down over-grown paths, calling and crying out.

Help! Help me, please!

She is seeking and searching.

Please.

In the seams of her sobbing, she begins to hear her mother's song. And now she is smelling and finally seeing, her mother as a light, as a ghost. She collapses to the ground breathless and desperate to do, to BE the that which is needed and to bring the young woman back to this life. The scent of her mother is strengthening. She feels the touch in her palm, and she holds tight to the hand and is gently pulled and falling down into the other place and Mother is there. Girl is desperate and frantic and way too fast. She vibrates with fear and anxiety and is neither here nor there and cannot see.

Mother is soft and kind and still. She sees the here and she knows the there. She sits with the injured young woman and with her unsteady daughter and fills the space around here with a calming energy, a leading to peace sort of energy. Slowly and slowly, she holds her daughter close and eases her into this place and comforts her. With touch she slows her daughter's shaking. With her gaze she guides Girl to breathe and to still her thoughts.

Now Girl is ready. Mother shows her the way. She instructs and supports and cautions and does note that Girl is just as she was with the wolves and the bull. Mother understands death. She knows the Bad Man well. And Mother knows that all peoples and all nations serve the whole. She cannot spare Girl from what is coming, so she loves her extra strong, with extra care.

Girl hugs her mother and touches her heart and makes the signs for gratitude and love and missing, but she is already moving, sliding down and up, back.

Her eyes fly open. She leaps to her feet and flying as fast as she can, she races back to the dying young woman.

***

Next to the young woman, Girl falls to her knees. She is too late. The young woman is dead.

Girl's head falls forward. Her breath has gone, knocked away and out of her by some tremendous blow. Sorrow and failure and surrender claim her body. She is falling and folding and going down.

No.

Girl says,

No.

She gathers herself and firms her heart and sits upright. Girl looks to the heavens and begins to work. In her haste, she does discount the pain.

***

She sings the songs and moves her hands and draws the shapes. She feels the thickness of the air changing. Girl is stirring and shaping and moving the air, the energies there. Sending life to the young woman and over and all around her, washing and willing the young woman to accept. Her moving hands collect and compress energy. It becomes thicker and denser until Girl sees air thick as smoke and tendrils tiny, ephemeral and wispy, moving and turning to cloud, thinner than a small birds soft feather, wending their way to young woman's nostrils and moving into and down and through. The young woman moves and begins to groan.

Pain comes with the delivery. Girl knows of this part but knowing is shallow, hollow and pale. To do resurrection means she must take on the pains of the fallen. It comes on fast and hard and quick as a hailstorm.

Girl gasps and feels the slash of Bad Man's knife, the warmth of the blood spilling out of her and the finality of meeting the ground, heavy and emptying of life. She feels the weight of his foot pressed into her throat and crushing down, down, and hurting her, hurting her in a way that is beyond physical. Her very heart is hurting and sad, questioning why, why, why and she will never know because she is dying. The Bad Man is using his foot to press down so that he can pull the knife from her chest. And Girl cannot even scream because her physical pain is crushed beneath the weight of her soul hurt and confusion.

The resurrected young woman is screaming in horror; coming back from the dead is not supposed to be. She is no longer confused and sad; she is only horrified and hurting and screaming and her mind is going and going.

Her eyes hold the vision of Bad Man slicing through her family like wind moving across the surface of still water. She sees everywhere, bodies dropping to the grass, and some are in agony, and some are gone so fast that they never feel themselves hitting dirt. The young woman gasps and shoves herself to an upright position and whips her head to the right and searching there sees her own child dead and gone as gone can be. The wail, the wash of it, swells up like some giant wave, heavy and towering and dark and smashing over her until she cannot breathe.

The young woman is gone and broken; it is irrevocable. Girl is shocked and retreats scrambling backwards with heels kicking and hands grasping to pull. Mother is gone from her. Instead, there, at the edge of the clearing, exactly on the border that separates forest from camp, is Bad Man.

He moves faster than he has in months, or years and he grasps the reanimated young woman's head and turning, turns it quick and sharp, down. There is a crack and limpness and gone-ness and the young woman is back where she belongs, where she longed to be.

Bad Man, for the first time since his love has passed, looks directly at Girl, and sees her. And Girl sees HIM. For interminable moments, the small family of two intently watch into the other. Thoughts of these terrible vengeful years and these long, lonely losses pass between them. There is love there and longing, but it cannot overcome the inevitability.

Yes, it can Father!

Bad Man's face returns to its mask. He is Death and turning; he is walking, leaving. And Girl, she is motionless and stunned and struck still.

Still.

A confusion comes, turbulent and swirling through her mind; she is dizzy with it and falling down onto her back, she closes her eyes and breathes.

What does this mean? Why had the Bad Man left a person hanging on the precipice for her to find, was it accidental, intentional? Why had he returned and watched as she brought the young woman back to consciousness and then killed her as quickly as it became apparent that she was mad and would never be human again?

Despair comes with the heaviness of a wet wool blanket. The sad clinging and grey, weighs on Girl's chest and presses her down onto the waiting earth and there she quickly falls asleep. She dreams of snakes and wizards and screams that echo through the insides of her. She feels the tearing, ripping separation as people depart this place not knowing of the next. And she knows only to go to the other place and speak with the Buffalo Man or perhaps her mother. She feels lost and alone and sad. Her confusion is a saving thing because if she had possessed any certainty, it would have been bleak and over and empty. Girl is blessed with confusion and so she sleeps.

Bad Man waits.

He cannot say why, it is only what he does, like breathing or blinking. He waits in the shadow of the thick, green, wood. The trees standing around him, their crowns reach high into the sky. Bad Man is well acquainted with their rough barky skin and their softly bobbing, evergreen arms. They do not speak to him. They do not judge him. The tree folk exist here as naturally as air. Without comment or criticism, they only watch.

Bad Man sits.

He could stay here for a moment or, just as easily, until his body dissolves into dirt. He imagines himself sitting quietly beneath these giants, motionless, watching, breathing, waiting until he becomes food for them and part of them and perhaps one day, he himself will be a small green needle on the end of a giant, bobbing up and down arm, of a giant, thousand-year-old tree.

This is Bad Man being still.

Night falls, clouds skate across the dark sky, wind blows and then sun comes, and Bad Man does see the Girl. His response is small, only an errant sip of air marks some slipping, internal clicking thing which is a wisp of feeling. As quickly as light comes it is gone, extinguished with a small hissing sound, same as of a spark, when doused in cold water.

Bad Man watches as Girl moves through the carnage he has left in his wake. But he sees only her.

He watches how she moves. He sees her feelings written on her face. He notes her surprise when she finds a living body and the urgency with which she attends the young woman. He watches Girl frantically run this way, then that, in a near panic as she seeks the materials necessary to keep the young woman alive.

He watches as the dead young woman comes back to awareness. He sees there is nothing but madness in her eyes.

He watches as Girl recoils from the insane young woman and scrambles backwards. And he does break from cover, leaving his observation place and rushing to the Girl and the mad young woman. His hands are a blur, and he is quick. Bad Man moves his hands and mercifully ends the young woman finally and forever. And Bad Man looks into Girl's eyes, and she thinks he is merciful in ending the young woman's mad suffering, forgetting that he is the one who allowed it. Girl does not see that the Bad Man's mercy extends only to her.

From his place of omniscient indifference, Bad Man experiences Girl and her electric pulsing large-ness. She is ground and dirt and sky and smoke, and he remembers when they first met, not her birth, not the crying nights. He remembers the morning she gazed up at him with her eyes clear and full of wonder.

He saw reflected there some piece, some less clouded place, bereft of any jaded, already knowing. Seeing her then, he himself was moved for a moment back into awe, reverence and surprise. And seeing this place, this life, this breath anew; he met his daughter. And in that moment, some bridge, some connection hung precariously above the blackest, bleakest, abyss deep, was sparked, made, built, and forged. And Bad Man was in that moment so completely captured that he did not think.

He remembers leading her to the cold water's edge and cupping his hands, filling them with water and bathing her small brown feet and seeing the thrill of delight as she felt the coldness of it. He remembers walking her forward until her feet immersed in the moving, clean, clear waters and then leading her farther out, deeper. He remembers Girl's gasping laughs as she, hesitant, grabbed hold of his arm, not for lack of footing but for balance none the less and security. He remembers feeling trusted and how that cracked something in him then.

He remembers exhaling.

The Bad Man remembers teaching Girl to swim and to hike and to build the fire, yes…. these functional necessities, but more importantly he remembers showing her how to lay on her back and softly watch the clouds float by, to fly in imagination with the swooping circling hawks and to see, really see, the ant people and their diligence and humility and perseverance.

Bad Man knows Girl will not stop.

She is incapable of cynicism, and her hope lies as strong in her breast as his self-loathing lies in his.

He turns and there is only an imperceptible pause before he strides into the safety of shadow and the company of the silent, nonjudgmental trees.

Vision Quest

Girl has lost the strength to stand.

She has fallen and sits staring numbly at her Not Father's back as he fades back into the shadow of the tree line. She will sit here, surrounded by devastation, numbly staring at the dirt, no thoughts in her head, until she can somehow hold the whole of what has happened inside herself.

She remembers all of it, the frenzied collecting of life saving herbs, followed by her seeing the inhuman madness lighting the young woman's eyes. She remembers the swiftness with which Bad Man had strode to the young woman. She remembers the knowing ease with which he had snapped the young woman's neck and ended her and her suffering.

She holds close, the one, too brief, look exchanged between her and the Bad Man. She remembers the eyes of her Father, visible for one moment and full of torment and horror. And then there was the dropping of his veil and only the soulless, the beyond salvation, the empty of the man remaining.

Girl sits and the day moves on and the night comes. She does not feel the chill or the hunger or the thirst. She only sits surrounded by the waste, the wreckage of an encampment and the bodies and the belongings and all they ever were, all they will never be, all strewn randomly, chaotically, and she does not stir. Girl can move only in, falling down and down into the dark.

Dawn comes and the sun peeks over the horizon blazing pink and red and orange and yellow and finally white hot and blinding. Girl feels the beginnings of hunger. Her lips are chapped and dry; still, she sits motionless, mind blank, face plain and without expression. Only small, far apart breaths indicate that she is a living creature and not just another body beginning to smell in this all dead place.

All through the glare, the bright light, the heat hot on her head and warm on her skin, through the salty remains of used to be sweat and tear, through the stiff and numb foreign-ness of her limbs, all through the buzzing of the frenzied flies and even until they are fat and slow, Girl sits still as a statue. She does not move, save for the odd strand of wispy hair fluttering tentatively against her forehead as if to gently ask her to awaken.

Girl sits. Girl breathes.

It turns late, and the sun going over the opposite horizon, is sliced into smaller and smaller pieces. Leaving the sky, sun is taking warmth and comfort with it. There is one last glorious spreading flaring of light, brilliant across the sky, that creates a glow in any cloud or on any towering peak and then, sun is gone.

Darkness steals Girl's remove and brings her back to here. With the darkness there comes a small, ancient apprehension that is unrelieved by flame. She re-enters the present and as she feels the chill and the pain and the hunger and the loneliness, Girl shivers. She does not move to stand or drink or eat, but her eyes are animated and alive now, rather than the flat void of her earlier, inwardly turned eye.

She sits through the night and rubs her legs and clenches and relaxes her muscles. She fidgets and feels her doubts flicker and build. The questions come.

Why me? Why am I here? What am I doing?

All through this night, this human night, this time of alone and floating and unmoored, where every sound seems an alarm and the stars drag slowly around the sky, Girl waits. She is no longer hungry. Her mouth is dry. Her lips are pulled back and stick to her teeth. She feels the pain of months of travel, the aches and the fatigue, the weary hurt of dehydration and Girl understands what she must do.

Stirring and attempting to stand, falling, and crawling past the dead young woman; she retrieves the drum and the rattle. Dragging herself over to a log she sits and begins to drum. She strikes a slow beat, and she tries to sing, but her throat will only whistle- crack a dry, high note. And so, Girl is silent of voice, only her hands and her heart keep the song going.

With the flat, rhythmic thumping of the drum, the night rolls back as if from a fire. The song is pushing the darkness out of the center of her and though tired and alone and tiny... finally, Girl is not afraid.

As the stars fade into grey, there is a slow stirring awakening, streamers of pink and fire snake across the skin of the sky, and birds call to one another and begin the gossip as is the way of their kind. Girl is drumming louder but the beat is intermittent and has no rhythm. She cannot sing but she can hear those who do. Their chanting fills her ears, and she tosses her hair and swings her head in time and the drumstick is driven by unseen hands and Girl is rising to her tired feet and shuffling.

Some low sounds crack forth and she is singing the song. Now dust puffs up around her feet where they strike the ground. Round and round she goes and there are wisps of others, and they join, and dance and chant and Girl is comforted. She has found a renewed strength and so she sings louder. And out of the fuzzy green early morning mist, Mother comes and rests her palm on Girl's forehead and leads her to a cool place and sits her down.

***

Medicine Woman Mother does not speak. She settles to the ground and spreads her skirt's folds out around her in a circle and then tucks the hems in carefully underneath her knees. She straightens her spine and places her hands carefully upon her knees. Once situated properly, in the correct shape, with the proper attention applied, Mother raises her gaze and looks directly into Girl Daughter.

Girl watches carefully and understands that this stark and detailed attention to posture is a collecting of her mother's whole person, a preparation, and she does follow her mother's lead and arranging just so and adjusting just so she raises her eyes to join her Medicine Woman Mother.

Girl is grateful for the straightness of her spine as the relaxation comes and gravity pulls her down and down, into the earth. Passing down, she smells the good clean earth and is tickled by the soft tendrils of fuzzy roots. Falling farther, inverting and plunging, plummeting down until down is up and breaking out into the other place's valley, Girl is travelling a familiar path. There are rising mountains on either side and there, the far away. There is a shimmering quality to the air and Girl instinctively reaches out to grasp her mother's hand and holding it warm, she closes her eyes. Tears slide out from under each of her delicate eyelids and burn soft, tracing tracks, silver down her face.

This is enough.

This is enough, I will not ask more, just to touch, just to hold Mother's hand, it is enough.

Reluctantly, she opens her eyes. Medicine Woman Mother is still here, smiling back with such tender fullness that Girl is encouraged to open her eyes wider. Taking in the slight glow, the slight blur, the indefinite edges and the definite warmth emanating from her mother, she is strengthened and steadied. Girl feels her toes and her feet sinking into the good dirt, and she feels her scalp being tugged gently towards the sky and glancing up startled she cannot name the color, she cannot describe the time of day only that it is now and that it is beautiful.

Softly now Girl brings her gaze back from the heavens and there is the smile on her face, on her mother's face, and the warmth of her hand gently tugging, pulling and they, the two of them, step and step and move.

The grasses are soft and smeared and golden brown mixed with greens and it is all so at once and confusing. But Mother Medicine Woman is smiling and guiding, and Girl is moving into this place.

Death.

What do I do with death Mother?

There is a body. We have a body, had a body. Someone has left their body and gone. Is life only an energy that can wink away and gone? Or, like all other magic, does life only transform and change. A body remains and changes, but some essential animating energy leaves and where does it go?

Girl is reaching, stretching and straining to hold death and grief and longing and joy and love and gone, gone forever gone and yet ...here.

She is trying to surround and support the idea that grief does not displace love and death does not erase life. She is here and there too, indistinct and blurred. Her skin seems to provide no barrier, inside and out are all and all the other. There are realities larger than the ones she knows and maybe more.

Mother waits and, with her presence, makes time for the organizing and the shattering and the re-arranging and the all-over-again losing and finally the finding.

Mother waits until the, scattered to the wind, pieces of Girl settle and fall into place like leaves fluttering down and arranging themselves into a sculpture, a moving, breathing being. This is human. And Human, upon stumbling into awareness, upon the scales falling from their eyes, is overcome with gratitude and the filling up and the spilling over.

This grateful awakening is such a movement of energies that the whole of reality stills and sighs in agreement that yes, this is so.

So, yes!

And more and magic, and this mystery revealed is that there is no distinction, no edge, no border, no end.

Girl considers here and there. And,

Is she a bridge or a wall? Does she connect or is she in fact the creator of the illusion of separateness? Is there a moving between? Or only a moving in more directions of the very same experience.

And Mother smiles.

The turned-up corners of her mother's mouth change their color. Her luminous eyes shift until there is the teacher, and the teacher is the buffalo, and the raven, and the wolf, the trees and the mother, too.

Constellations track across the inky sky and Girl feels them fall and land on her flesh and there is no burning like before. They move across her skin and arrange upon her in such a way.

There is teacher and they are building and constructing Medicine Girl's understanding. She is swept away in time, sucked from the shore, and pulled far out into a deep, vast, endless ocean. There are the darkness-es and the light, the swell and fall, the ever-changing shorelines and all the myriad real, responses to the moon and the sun and all the heavens.

There are ceremonial knowings, and elemental truths. There are ancestors and beings that defy explanation or even description. Girl is become Medicine Woman. She straddles the center place that some find as an impenetrable veil.

To, with her very own hands, feel the shape of suffering... she suffers. To know evil, she does do evil and to understand compassion she is tossed lost, adrift without any way to save herself, until the nations collude and pull her to safety and bathe her and do feed her and deliver her drink.

And to know love she is become Mother and father and lover and child, and she does "die" to this place and "walk" in that one and moving between, she only is.

Medicine Woman sighs.

Return

There is no more up…. or down.

Medicine Woman does not emerge from any else, other or where. She is one moment sitting quietly and the next softly watching all that is around her.

The long dead bodies have turned to bone. The campsite is gone, turned to dust, gone to seed, returned to what it was before and what it will always be. For long moments, hours, days perhaps, Medicine Woman sits and breathes. Her eyes are swirling galaxies of brilliant color, her hair has streaks of grey and the swirling constellations of power coil and spiral and line her skin. She is no longer a young girl.

Medicine Woman sits inside the folding, overlapping confusion of time and place. Her Mother is here and there and gone and a head turn away and the ache of it, the heart squeezing pain of it is not to be feared or turned away from. Medicine Woman is larger than fear and larger than this hurt and so can clearly see, Love. She considers that Love may be the center that holds all the strands and streamers of this great play together. We are all, all at once, the old woman with her aches and foggy vision and the child who dances for the joy of moving. We are the pain of birth giving way to the hard, anvil heavy, weight of grief that presses down and crushes the very breath from our chests.

We carry-contain the swelling pressure behind our eyes that forces tears to slide hot down our faces, tears that come with falling, falling without hope of rescue into love, into a chasm, into the next unknown.

Medicine Woman sits in the center and sighs and the grasses bend towards her and the birds change their songs.

She rises to her feet. It is time to find her father.

Woman smoothes her hands down and over and shakes her hair to settle it soft and heavy on her shoulders. Standing straight as smoke on a windless day, she tilts her face to the sky and opens her palms to the out, the around. The sweetest, kindest smile grows, grooves into her face. The power signs scroll and soothe around her skin, twining and rearranging and there is some dance there, some earthy phenomenon as primary as cloud and storm. She turns in a small circle, softening and radiating the who of her, the essential of her and it is a calling.

Eagle, high in the sky, hears and wheels to fall gracefully in her direction and Woman feels her heart soar to the blue sky and lifting, raise her up on her toes with the ecstasy of flight and connection. Eagle carves a turn and Medicine Woman lifts her arms as though they are wings and carves the very same turn. They, the two of them, Eagle, and Medicine Woman, feel the air thick beneath them supporting flight. And the whole world is higher, raised up into the clouds as a consciousness, witnessing its own play and dance.

Eagle slowly presses down on the air and is off, in search of Bad Man. Medicine Woman follows.

The Old Bad Man

He sits heavy and tired. He is bone deep fatigue. The Old Man's life has etched its own symbols of power into his face, and onto his body, wrinkles, and scars and too much sun, too much cold and too much horror. He sits heavy. He has built his own symbols of power. Every knife wound, bullet hole, burn mark and clawed place creates his personal story of power and nature.

Old Man sits on a rock, head hanging down, forearms draped over his knees, too tired to even fight gravity. He is pulled low and droopy as a late summer willow. Too long without water. Too much, too many, too long, life.

He stares past the dry, brown grass and through the dusty powdered dirt, down and down into the space below. He stares into the faces of those he has murdered and tortured and terrified and ended and sent to the next place in every terrible way imaginable. There are old men like himself and young people, children and women who seem more bewildered and confused than scared or angry.

There are warriors who stare back wanting one more chance to kill him, to tear his heart from his chest and push his lifeless body over the final edge with a disdainful foot.

This Old Bad Man can barely find the path, the thin, worn, long ago way back to how he came to be. It is overgrown with weed and thankfully unused by animals and so fading, it is hidden, as it should be. He is at once grateful that no one else has come this way and sad that he cannot follow it home to himself.

Here, with the sun hot on his back, he longs for its warmth to penetrate and warm his soul, but it does not. The burning goes only skin deep. He is cold inside in a way that no fire can change, no sun can repair.

The Old Bad Man exists in a strange, timeless limbo, for him the idea of tomorrow or yesterday is as remote as the silver sliver of moon, washed over and hidden by drifting clouds in the night. Yet, of late, he has turned in his saddle more and more frequently, spinning in place and folding forward from the waist, leaning forward, and staring long into the distance behind to see who is following him. He can feel a presence, a weight, and occasionally he will feel a small, thin branch falling back into place, movement where none should be.

And then too, there is this fog, a sort of permanent dissolution of the real, smearing the edges of his vision and greying the light and whispering. He hears his Woman's voice, and it is unnerving, unsettling to him. She calls him to life, reminding him of places inside himself that have been in shadow for so long that he had long ago stopped even arguing for their existence. Shooing away these whispers as if waving away gnats, he moves and shifts. At least there is this, he has come to the end of his purpose. There is only one person left alive who can be traced back to his love's end. One last coal to extinguish. One last light to snuff.

This Old Bad Man does not feel elation at the prospect. There is only a small flickering shadow in his mind as this information falls into its place. One more. Once more.

Horse does not eat much these days. He has lost the taste for food. As he, Horse, feels the end click into the old man's mind, he flicks his tail and turns his head slightly to look. For a hundred years and more they have traveled together. In the beginning it was fast and ferocious and violent and filled with an energy of its own. Lately, the in between times, the tracking and hunting and finding times, have gotten longer and longer, pauses so long that life has started creeping back into their days. No longer surfing the energy of hate, Old Bad Man has begun to notice colors and sounds in spite of himself.

He notices the clarity of chilled water and its laughter as it spills over the round, grey and green rocks. He notices when waking, the drops of dew that rest on his eyelids. And Bad Man feels the thrill and the sharp intake of breath that fills him up when the cold-water splashes high and around away from the dancing steps of Horse. Drops of icy cold-water land and stick, sparking like jewels on his skin.

He notices the flashing goosebumps racing across his skin when quail explode from hiding and beat the air so furiously that it hurts his ears with the vibrations. He notices these things. And now comes the awareness, the purpose almost lost, almost gone, almost gone, one to go and the whispers, and the rustling in the night. The Old Bad Man sits up and stares into the dancing flames and farther, into the ember, the glowing oranges shifting to black and back. And Bad Man ponders ends and edges.

***

Old Bad Man feels the pulsing of the earth as it breathes and shifts. And he knows the magnetic pull of north and south, east, and west and the last one he must kill.

Old Bad Man straightens his back, and his hands fall from his knees. He lowers himself to his knees and creaking and cracking, popping like the dried twigs and branches on the forest floor, betraying presence, he growls an exhale and falls to his side and drifts.

Medicine Woman stares out into the dark. She smells the Bad Man's fire and the sadness and death and Bad Man himself. And, though it cannot be true, she maybe sees a small distant glimmer from a fire that does not warm the soul, and only barely warms the skin.

Dawn comes.

The fire has long gone cold.

There is a lightening of the darkness, a greying, a stirring of leaves, and the birds wake and watch. When the first, flashing ray of light comes peeking over the horizon, they begin to sing and chatter and call the day to life. Old Bad Man sits upright and scrubs the sleep from his face with his dry calloused palms. His hair is thin and wispy white and missing in places where he has been touched by stone or steel and only scar remains.

The morning light leaves dark hollows and highlights, protruding cheeks and bridge of nose. His eyes glitter dark and deep, and it seems they are awash in suffering and sadness, and cruelties and all of the flavors of a long life spent on vengeance. He is already gazing west and sniffing and licking his dry lips and scuffing his feet in the dry, dusty grass. Horse flicks his tail and blows through his nostrils. His head hangs low and close to the ground as if grazing, but he is not, he will not.

Old Man pushes himself heavily to his feet and limps over to Horse. They were young once and cruel and then in love and then empty save for a single purpose and now, soon, they will be empty again. It is the best to hope for, not relief nor joy, just a finish, done and complete. And in this narrowing and collecting of possibility there is a fatalistic comfort. This is what must happen. This is what will happen.

***

Medicine Woman is awake. She breathes the cool morning air, pulling it deep, in through her skin and hands and feet and she stands in prayer, which for her is an expression of gratitude and connection.

Eagle sits perched proudly on a nearby bough. He is fierce and he sees well, and he does not second guess. Eagle is certain. He has found the Bad Man and led the Woman here as requested. All that remains are these final few miles.

Medicine Woman turns in the direction of her father, her palms are wide and face the earth. They listen carefully to the pulsing waves there. She is still and quiet inside and wonders if today she will end her father or if he will end her. There can be no more madness. This trail has exhausted all reason and is down to this, he will stop. She will stop him.

She moves in the direction Eagle indicates. She goes efficient, swinging forward in that way of people who travel by foot, the rhythm merging with her surroundings, her feet soft upon the ground. The trees all sigh and the animal nations still. Some elemental meeting is in the making and all feel the density of it sparking an extra brilliance in the colors of the forest, an extra crispness to the puffs of dust that burst underfoot. Even the birds stop their singing and sit on the branches that provide some shade and some shelter from the swirling breezes that are building.

Old Bad Man can feel the wave building behind him. The pressure is like a weight pressing on his back urging him to move faster and yet, he does not. He is caught in the same giant expression of inevitability as is the Medicine Woman as is the Young Man and his lover wife and their unborn child. The Great Wheel turns and no one can stop it. And so, he moves towards his final act of hate, and he longs for the release of it and holds no hope for salvation, only an end.

Medicine Woman feels his acceptance and hurries forward.

There is a small valley. It is filled with love and life and the joy of gratitude and new consciousness. And now Medicine Woman understands where her Not Father is going.

Medicine Woman gasps in her chest and feels a small hurt there, an aching sadness tinged with fear and loathing and shame. She begins to accelerate her speed. She knows she will not be fast enough.

So very confusing.

Medicine Woman steps to the in between of two giant pines. Down slope there is a valley, cut through by a stream that ordinarily dances and sparkles and laughs aloud; today there is only a waiting. She feels the hitch, the stutter in her breath, in her heart. There is a Young Man and a clearly pregnant Woman going about their morning and the connection between them is tangible to the point of having density and substance. There is life emanating outward and it is in hard contrast to the still space where her Father is moving.

Medicine Woman can see, she can feel the twining, the eddying, swirling combination of time and gravity and storm. These elemental forces are the source from which her symbols derive; the symbols, they are the very shape of power. The turning and spilling into and pressing into, the circling and spiraling back into the spaces left behind, these are the magics, these are the mysteries and the story. These symbols were once burned into her father's skin and her mother's and hers, too. Now they are etched as scars, as marks left by life, wrinkles and sadness-es and laughs and passions, all the human energies. These marks are the evidence of a magical life.

Medicine Woman knows she is too far from the valley to stop what is coming, too far to even cry out a warning and yet she tries. She tries with all of her being. Reaching into her center, tearing loose power that has long lay dormant, Medicine Woman screams into the valley and the trees themselves tremble and the small mammals freeze, but there is no stopping the Bad Man. There is no stopping the turning of the wheel.

***

She watches with a fascination so thorough that it tastes, is colored even, in shades approaching admiration. There is a pure thing here. The Old Bad Man is an undiluted, doubt free being. Medicine Woman can feel the pull towards the relief of certainty and respite from the haunting unknown. She shakes it off and hurries even more.

She sees the Young Man fall and there is a stopping. For a moment, the whole valley is still. Her Father, the Bad Man, bursts forth from the tree line. He is a terrible force and filled with his evil certainty. He is become elemental. And he is streaking towards the Young Man who has already fought his way back to his feet and is grasping and pulling at the arrow embedded in his body. It is too little and too late, and he is clubbed hard and goes limp, falling to the earth, empty of animation and consciousness. The Bad Man has not even slowed. He is in full sprint, his blurred track curving to the young woman there.

Gasping with the shock of it, Medicine Woman sees the unimaginable. The young woman has drawn her blade and is moving towards Bad Man with a certainty of her own. And this coming collision, this hard war between two opposites, between the life and the death of it, the beginning and the end of it, is the whole turning and spinning of the great wheel held in a moment.

Medicine Woman cannot follow the tracks of their knives. The killing is all too fast. But she does see the clicking into place, the understanding, that death has won in the end, on both being's faces. Her Father staggers to a stop and falls to his knees. The young woman, astonishingly and beyond comprehension, continues forward and ends Bad Man's life even as he is ruining her body and taking the future away from her and her never born girl child. The valley of laughter and love, life and dreams is no more. There is left only a place of unspeakable tragedy. There remains only a sad hollow, question.

Why?

The answers all spill warm and rusty red, onto the grass and into the dirt.

Why even ever start if all ends here anyway?

The questioning is not the Bad Man's. the questioning is not the dead young woman's nor the life that never had a chance to be. The questioning is Medicine Woman's and she, awakening to her own presence and there-ness, explodes into motion. Flying down the side of the valley, as fast as light from the sky and leaving, the loud booming, cracking, thunder and now. Now she has her own sort of knowing and purpose. Arriving, flying into the meadow there, the blood is all on the dirt; there is no more moving forth and out of the bodies of the gone.

Young Man has regained awareness. It is no good thing. He staggers to his feet and falls towards his love, in hurried, halting, desperate, steps.

Medicine Woman watches as the Young Man, broken, slows and stills, his hands still patting the air as he tries to put back that which can never be put back. And She is taking him and turning him and making sure that he will live. Turning to the young woman and unborn child she gathers them together in her arms and wills life into them, and it passes around their bodies as water around river rock and moves into the essential them and fills them up.

The young woman, holding her baby, is turning in confusion now. Medicine Woman reaches, touching, taking her hand, and holding the three of them. Falling down and down and into the next valley, the next place, and midwifing them, guiding them, and the exhaling here, becomes the inhaling there, and confusion is changing to joy with only a moment of, a winking light of, loss or transition.

Medicine Woman inhabits all these places and all these nows at once. Holding them is a part of her wisdom and compassion and love and she is moving more fully into the place where her father lays. The life is still easing out of his body as it is relaxing into its last shape. His symbols, the scars and the wrinkles, all the evidences of life are leaving him. He is smoothing and softening.

Coming fully back into this now, this place, she is standing watching this thing, this corpse and the coagulating and thickening and stiffening and she is again lost in some sort of fascination.

How did he? Why did he?

And she is holding the times, when together they moved barefoot through the soft summer grasses and lay upon their backs staring up and watching the clouds turn into stars. She is remembering the softness of his warm hand holding her as she leans out over the edge of the precipice and he lends her the confidence to lean farther, to see farther, to be larger than she ever believed she could be.

Medicine Woman is seeing him again, pause, staring closely into her eyes, before turning away and going back into the trees. She is watching the shifting, cracking, earth-quaking on his face as he struggles to kill the human inside himself. She kneels next to his body and tentatively reaches out and caresses his bitter, old man cheek with the back of her hand and she feels the whole of it. The young woman and child and the Bad Man and death and she takes his hand and stands next to him for a moment, there in his moment of confusion, as he arrives in his new place. She would strike him down there and there and follow him from world to world and place to place and kill him over and over again until what?

And so, instead, she touches her hand to his chest and smiles a sad, tender smile.

In such a way, The Great Wheel turns.

Medicine Woman sighs and returns to the place and time of the Young Man and begins the work...

Epilogue

Gratitude

The flap is thrown open. Heat rushes out and loses, is lost, to the night-time chill. Thick cold air pours into the lodge and the young warrior and Medicine Woman are immersed in the coolness, submerged in the cleanliness and they rest.

Outside, the sacred fire burns low. The white-hot glow of the ancestor stones, shimmers, and sighs. Kind, warm light peeks into the lodge, staying near the doorway as an uncertain guest.

Young Warrior looks upon Medicine Woman and notes that her face shines brighter than the dying fire. Perhaps the flames there, that heat the rocks, are themselves only a reflection of the light she emits. She sits seemingly timeless, tireless and eternal. She is mother and woman, wife and Creatress...she is Medicine Woman.

Young Warrior feels a word begin and,

Shhh....

She is quieting him.

No words. Just breathe.

***

The young warrior sits.

He sees the steam rising and swirling away from his skin. There in the collision of heat and cold and human moisture a small fog is created and drifting away. Dissipating and dissolving, the ethereal sweat carries some rage in its droplets that *poof,* are soon gone. Perhaps the dark seething tracks of rage and vengeance and hatred float away with the mist and vanish.

But.

Grief does not.

The pain of loss... does not.

As bewilderment and awe begin to wane, as magic leaves the lodge like heat, the young warrior's pain is felt again. Young Warrior, to his surprise, is weeping and wept. Tears stream unremarked down his face and a bone deep sadness consumes his light.

This time, it is Medicine Woman who goes to the small remaining fire and with the singed poplar rake moves the last of the ancestors into the stone depression in the center of the lodge. She brings in her herbs and the water and gourd and places them carefully. She strikes on the drum and Young Warrior is jarred back to the moment. She waves her hand, and the door flap falls.

It is dark.

Moments pass in silence. Eyes adjust and spines adjust. The heat is back.

The two weary travelers sit silent and watch until they can see the stones, the ancestor's glow. The super-heated rocks radiate white and orange light and black lines ripple and dance on their skins. The ancestors and their waving luminescence point to a way, a direction of travel to turn one's eyes. The white, orange, yellow beckons and Young Warrior follows. He watches deeper and deeper into the translucent stones and their dancing light. Medicine Woman at just the right moment, drops herbs on the stones that incinerate and vanish as first a flash of bright and then a black speck on the orange red skin, there for a blink, then gone.

Medicine Woman passes a drum and stick to Young Warrior and taking up her own, sets a rhythm, a call, and she begins to sing.

For an awfully long time, a length of time, the Young Warrior does not hear the medicine words. The steady beat and resonance are enough, and they carry him back and forward and out, until it seems the veils are no more. Here and now and there and then and soon or not are no longer separate. IS only IS.

Amongst the people and all the relations, nations, and all and all, there sounds the most immense song ever sung. The words began before there was speech or the elk call, before bird song even. It is at first a vast silence, an uninhabited dark... then wind and thunder, and great, groaning tectonic symphonies. Slowly it builds and adds and includes, a swelling song, sung by infinite voices, filling infinite space.

A sound that has no edge.

The song we call the voice of God,

Increasing in volume and louder and loud!

Silence.

And Medicine Woman has ceased her drumming.

And the stones speak their wordless tales.

Temporal experience and a sack of values are born, live and die and over and over. Pain and Love and Fear and the knowing the seasons brings no comfort, no comfort at all.

Wisdom is a dust that chokes closed our throats. We sit and seek order and explanation, understanding, but there are none that we temporal creatures can contain. Rising and falling, In and out, are all there is, and this is... inconceivable,

Even to stone.

And the ancestors go quiet.

Medicine Woman and Young Warrior gaze across the space and time and see each other, witness the being of each other as indescribably beautiful.

So, she pours the water and quenches the stones and steam fills the space and soaks into the skin and knowing is passed along from rock to water to human, and though it is no comfort, it is transformation and larger and holding what was seen.

We are both the singer and the song.

The End

DISCLAIMER

This is a work of **fiction**. Unless otherwise indicated, all the names, characters, places, events and incidents in this book are either the product of the author's imagination or **used in a fictitious manner**. Any resemblance to actual persons, living or dead, or actual events is purely coincidental.

Made in the USA
Coppell, TX
26 June 2021

58130233R00173